Simon exhaled as he ~~~ say good-bye." His vo~~~

Hannah stared at the moon. She would never sit here beside him again in this garden. *"There are no good-byes in the kingdom of heaven,"* she whispered, hoping her words carried the conviction her soul lacked.

Praise for *Torn Asunder* by Alana Terry

*"Filled with suffering, yet ultimately has a **resounding message of hope**."* ~ Sarah Palmer, Liberty in North Korea

*"Alana has a **great heart for the persecuted church** that comes out in her writing."* ~ Jeff King, President of International Christian Concern

*"Faith and love are tested beyond comprehension in this **beautifully written Christian novel**."* ~ Kathryn Chastain Treat, Allergic to Life: My Battle for Survival, Courage, and Hope

*"**Not your average love story** - wrapped in suspense, this story of faith will stop your heart as you hope and weep right along with the characters."* ~ Nat Davis, Our Faith Renewed

*"Torn Asunder is an **enthralling, heart-aching novel** that calls your heart to action."* ~ Katie Edgar, KTs Life of Books

The characters in this book are fictional. Any resemblance to real persons is coincidental. No part of this book may be reproduced in any form (electronic, audio, print, film, etc.) without the author's written consent.

Torn Asunder
Copyright © 2014 Alana Terry
978-1-941735-05-3

Cover design by Damonza.

Scriptures quoted from THE HOLY BIBLE, NEW INTERNATIONAL VERSION®, NIV® Copyright © 1973, 1978, 1984, 2011 by Biblica, Inc.® Used by permission. All rights reserved worldwide.

The hymns *My Jesus, I Love Thee* and *It Is Well* are in the public domain.
All other song lyrics copyright Cherie Norquay.
Used by permission.
www.cherienorquay.com

www.alanaterry.com

Torn Asunder

a novel by Alana Terry

"When you walk through the waters, I will be with you, and when you pass through the rivers, they will not sweep over you. When you walk through the fire, you will not be burned. The flames will not set you ablaze. For I am the Lord, your God, the Holy One of Israel, your Savior."
Isaiah 43:2-3

AUTHOR'S PREFACE

I first heard about a group of secret North Korean missionaries in a *Voice of the Martyrs* newsletter several years ago. I was impressed at the young ages of these underground workers and at the courage they showed going back *into* North Korea when everybody would agree the most logical route would be *out* of such a brutal country.

The other aspect of their ministry that jumped out to me was that these missionaries were to travel alone. After months of training together, they would have to cross the border and continue their ministry solo for their own safety. I didn't know it at the time, but the seeds for my third North Korea novel had just been planted.

The students I read about were sent over the border years ago. I do not know if any survived. I do not know if any were imprisoned. But I do know that the God who sustains them in their trials is the same God watching over Christians the whole world over.

If *Torn Asunder* is my first novel you've read, I'd like to welcome you. *Torn Asunder* shares a few characters introduced in other novels, but it can be read completely as a standalone. If you have read *The Beloved Daughter*, you may recognize a few of the people who play into this story you are about to enjoy. They are several years younger than you remember them, however, since the events in *Torn Asunder* take place while Chung-Cha is a teenager in Camp 22.

My heart has, from the beginning of my writing, been with Christians in the underground church, where the gospel is prohibited, where our brothers and sisters face imprisonment for their faith. My prayer is that this fictional story will help encourage those of us in the free world to worship God more fully, share his truth more boldly, and love our neighbors more passionately, as each day brings us closer to Christ's glorious returning.

ALANA TERRY

PART 1

CHAPTER 1

"Do you think it's all right to lie?" Hannah kicked the empty hammock and watched it swing lazily back and forth.

Simon bent down to pluck a stray weed near the base of a blood-red rose bush. "I guess it depends on why you're asking."

Hannah ran the tip of her tongue across her dry lip. "I was thinking about the Sterns' instructions. When we get back home, we're supposed to make up answers if anyone questions us. Is that really what God would want us to do?"

Simon's shoulder was almost close enough to touch hers, and she could sense the rise and fall of his chest without having to look. "Wrong or right, times may come when we have to stretch the truth. You know that, don't you?"

She stared at her hands. "But it's wrong."

He made a sound that was a blend between a chuckle and a sigh. "With everything ahead of us, you're worried about your conscience?" She couldn't tell if he meant to compliment her or not. After a pause, he turned until his face was so close she could smell the garlic and vinegar on his breath and the faint scent of American soap lingering on his skin. "If we want to survive, we need to be wise like serpents, just like Jesus said. As soon as we cross that river tomorrow, everything will change. We have to be prepared. If not ... well, then the Sterns might have wasted their time training us."

Hannah's arm brushed against his shirt. "But you wouldn't lie about your faith, would you?"

"Lie about being a Christian? I hope not."

"You hope not? What about that missionary Mrs. Stern mentioned who recanted to avoid the prison camps?"

Simon's features softened. "Mr. Stern told me something last week. He told me, 'Never judge someone who fails a test you yourself have yet to pass.'"

As Hannah thought of the hundreds of kilometers and sleepless nights ahead of her, she wondered what tests they would have to endure once they left the Secret Seminary.

Simon exhaled as he stretched his arms. "I wish we didn't have to say good-bye." His voice was distant. They had already discussed it before. There was nothing more to say. The Sterns insisted it was far too dangerous for the graduates to return to North Korea together.

Hannah stared at the moon. She would never sit here beside him again in this garden. "There are no good-byes in the kingdom of heaven," she whispered, hoping her words carried the conviction her soul lacked.

***

Juliette Stern stared out the window. She had been up in the den cleaning all afternoon. Everything needed to look perfect for the graduation ceremony tomorrow. The students had worked so hard. They had already sacrificed so much. They deserved a proper sending-off celebration. Heaven knew when they would have opportunity to rejoice together with other believers once they left Yanji.

She wiped the window with a paper towel, and her heart squeezed inside her chest just a little bit when she saw Hannah and Simon below in the garden. He leaned toward her so expectantly, so hopefully. A serene smile spread across her face. Did either of them know what was about to happen — what freedoms they would give up when they crossed the Tumen River and returned to the land of persecution and starvation? Juliette admired them, admired the courage it took to accept the call to sneak back to North Korea, but she wondered if sending them out really was the right thing. Especially with Hannah. She was so young. Juliette and her husband tried to talk to her about staying behind. Out of all the North Korean refugees who went through their Secret Seminary, Hannah was the most passionate about returning home. Nothing the Sterns could say would change her mind.

Juliette looked around to inventory all the work still left to be done for the graduation. She knew this den might be the last glimpse of refuge, the last taste of home, some of the students would ever experience.

CHAPTER 2

"I'm looking for Jesus in glory to come, from glory land over the sea."
The sound of lapping water interrupted Hannah's quiet song. She strained her ears. Was someone nearby? If they came after her, she had to be ready. She adjusted her bag. It was lighter after she gave away her food to the street children back at the bus stop.

The breeze was picking up. Hannah needed to move, but she couldn't stop wondering about Simon. Was he already across the border? Would he make it all right? Would she? She had always relied on his wisdom. What would she do now they were apart? She could still hear his voice in her mind. *"Never judge someone who fails a test you yourself have yet to pass."* Did either of them really know what tests lay ahead of them?

The last time she was at the Tumen River, she was a refugee, starving and terrified, fleeing the hunger and famine of her childhood. She tiptoed to the water's edge. The river flowed lazily. It was never very deep this time of year. A few steps, and she would be to the other side. Had the same water lapped Simon's feet when he crossed?

She sucked in her breath when her bare foot met the icy cold. She thought of the woman she had given her boots to a few hours ago back in Yanji. She didn't regret helping the young mother out, but now Hannah's thighs throbbed. The thin muscle on the front of her shins felt as tight as a piece of elastic about to snap, but she had to keep going. A little farther into the riverbed, she still hadn't shaken the feeling of being watched. Was that a twig breaking behind her? She spun around. *An animal*, she assured herself. *Just a little, harmless animal.*

"*A cloud of bright angels to carry me home ...*"

A few more unsteady steps brought her to the other side. One year ago, Hannah had risked border police and prison camps for a small taste of freedom in China, but she had never forgotten her homeland. She filled her lungs with the cool North Korean air and was surprised at how familiar it felt. She was home.

"*Yes, this will be heaven to me.*"

The song always reminded her of Simon. Even now, she could almost hear him singing with such conviction and power, never once suspecting he was hopelessly out of tune. But that was Simon. Bold. Courageous. Wherever he was right now, he certainly wasn't jumping and startling at every sound in the night. He'd hurry to complete the first phase of his mission without wondering about his own safety. Not like Hannah. She didn't know how much time she had already wasted staring into the darkness, hoping for strength just to move into the woods after crossing the river.

She had memorized over a dozen verses about fear at the Secret Seminary. Mrs. Stern told her to recite the passages to herself whenever she felt anxious. But even when she set her mind on Scripture, all she could think about was him, the way he talked, the way he smelled when he sat next to her for breakfast around the Sterns' big table. She remembered their conversation yesterday, the last night they spent in Yanji. She hadn't been able to sleep and wandered into Mrs. Stern's garden. Simon was reclining on the hammock, a Bible propped open against his chest, and she realized there was only one reason she had come out of her room at all.

It had nothing to do with fresh air or flowers.

"I thought you might still be awake." His smile had a disarming way of drawing all of her blood to her cheeks.

She sat across from him on the bench and eyed his Bible. "What are you studying?"

"Isaiah. Listen to this." He shone his little flashlight on the page and read, *"It is too small a thing for you to be my servant to restore the tribes of Jacob and bring back those of Israel I have kept. I will also make you a light for the Gentiles, that you may bring my salvation to the ends of the earth."*

Simon's voice soared with a wave of conviction that caused both yearning and aching to swell up in her spirit. He went on for several more verses. "Don't you see?" He sat up. Hannah focused on his exact inflection. Once they left the Secret Seminary tomorrow, would she ever hear his voice again? "Isn't it marvelous?" he asked.

She had missed everything he mentioned about the passage but nodded in agreement.

He closed the Bible and frowned. "Is something wrong?"

She pursed her lips together and looked at the stars. Would the sky look the same once she returned home? She was such a different person now. She realized that Simon was waiting for her and fumbled for a reply. "Just having a hard time sleeping, I suppose."

He stretched his back, arching it to one side and then the other, nearly toppling out of the hammock. He cleared his throat twice, but the second time sounded more like a squeak. "Actually, since we're both awake, there's something I wanted to ask you."

She focused on her slippers and didn't dare raise her eyes to his. One of Simon's vertebrae popped as he twisted his spine once again. She sucked in her bottom lip and glanced up at him. "Yes?"

He froze mid-stretch. His mouth hung half open, and deep red flushed its way up to his ears. "It's just that, well, I'm not exactly sure how to say this." He stood up awkwardly. It wasn't until then she realized how sweaty her palms had grown. With a heavy sigh, he sank to the bench beside her and crossed his arms. "I just wanted to tell you that I think you're very brave. Being the only girl to graduate the program, I mean."

Hannah stared into her lap and let out the breath she had been holding. "Thank you."

An owl screeched once, interrupting Hannah's memories. When would she stop acting so silly? She had work to do. There wasn't time to stand around all night reminiscing about someone she would never see again. She couldn't let the Sterns down. As she walked, she recited the directions she had memorized earlier.

She bit her lip. Were those leaves crunching? She braced herself for an attack that never came. After a few moments of perfect stillness, she looked up at the night sky and unclenched her jaw. At the rate she was going, she would never make it to her first stop before morning. Her bare feet were dripping wet, and the icy chill traveled through her veins up her aching legs.

It didn't take her long to reach the right house. Finding the courage to approach it was another matter. Why had the Sterns thought she could do this? She was only a child, really, not even twenty. And here she was, staring at a cabin she lacked the courage to approach, snapping her head around at every strange noise.

Even though I walk through the valley of the shadow of death, I will fear no evil, for you are with me; your rod and your staff, they comfort me.

The passage promised peace and protection, but Hannah felt neither. Staring at the house, she wondered what sort of comfort she'd experience if National Security agents arrested her the moment she knocked on the door.

She stared a little longer and prayed for God's help. Morning wouldn't wait. Besides, Simon and the others had probably each received much more dangerous missions than hers. How hard could it be to drop off some supplies with a known believer? If she ever saw Simon again, she didn't want to be ashamed of failing. As it was, she probably could have made her first two deliveries by dawn if she hadn't wavered for so long. Now she would have to wait a whole day before meeting her next contact.

Crouching in the woods, she drank the last drops of her water and saved the empty bottle for later. Making as little noise as possible, she felt for the hidden zipper in her backpack and took out several of the books and devices. After tucking them into the vest beneath her sweater, she slid the backpack under a bush and covered it with leaves and twigs. It was time. If she wanted to back out, she should have thought of that before she left Yanji and crossed the border in the first place. Holding her breath, she rushed ahead as though she might die if she didn't run fast enough.

A candle flickered inside the house, and the front door slipped open before she even reached the porch. She sucked in her breath, half prepared to see a National Security agent inside aiming a gun at her forehead.

"Come in, friend." Mr. Tong was a full head shorter than Hannah, with deep furrows etched into his ancient face. His back curved over his cane, and his whole body swayed in slow, almost melodic gyrations. He groped in front of him until he found Hannah's hand. "Forgive me, but I do my best seeing with these." His grip hinted at a strength long since departed as he ran his thumbs across Hannah's skin. "I have not had a visitor this young in many years." He moved aside and gestured toward a chair near the back of the room. "And where is your partner?"

Hannah frowned. "I came alone."

He tilted his head to the side. "A young man was with you, no?" He squinted his eyes and leaned out the door.

Hannah licked her lower lip. "No, I'm here by myself." Simon might be in a completely different province by this time tomorrow. Would she ever stop wondering what became of him?

Mr. Tong tapped the side of his head. "You bring bread for

me, no?" His shirt hung loose like a second set of skin, and his collarbone protruded through the cloth like a mountain ridge.

She thought about the little flower-swallows she had given all her food packs to before she crossed the Tumen River into North Korea. The street children had been so enthusiastic, rushing up to her, hanging onto her limbs. As soon as she emptied the front of her backpack, they were gone. "I'm sorry. I don't have any food with me."

He smiled. "Not food, child. Bread. Living Word. You have brought me the Word of God, no?"

Embarrassed, she took one of the audio devices and placed it in his outstretched palms. He felt the small machine and nodded, fingering the complex parts. "I can show you how it works," she offered.

Mr. Tong shook his head. "There is no need. But I thank you for this treasure, child. It was just last week that I gave away my last player. That was one of the reasons I knew you would be coming, understand."

Hannah didn't understand, but she set the other units on the table in front of him. "I have four here all together. I wish it were more."

Mr. Tong's swaying grew even more pronounced. "A treasure, child."

"I also brought you these." Hannah slid the books out from her vest and placed them in his outstretched hands.

His milky eyes widened, and a smile cracked through the maze of wrinkles and creases on his face. He opened one of the Bibles and sniffed the pages loudly. "Manna from God Almighty." He brought the book to his cheek and caressed its cover.

"I hope it's enough." She stood up.

He held the Bibles so tightly the veins in his forearms popped up like blue riverbeds. "There will never be enough. We pass out one Bible; ten people get saved. So then we need ten more Bibles, no? But why are you standing? Sit down. You have had a long journey, and I have expected you."

Mr. Tong reached out, found Hannah's hand, and pulled her back down onto the chair. With nimbleness despite his age, he made his way to the stove and grabbed two teacups. "You see, as soon as I ran out of the audio players, I knew you would be coming. I thought to myself, *My visitors will be cold and thirsty.* So I prepared you a treat." She already recognized the smell of ginseng tea. Her stomach growled. He placed a small cup in front of her, along with a plate of pickled vegetables. "For you." He smiled when she took her first bite, and she wondered with embarrassment if he could tell how hungry she was just by listening to her eat.

He brought his own mug over. "It is good, no?" He grunted as he sat down. "The ginseng is not easy to find, but today is a day to celebrate. It has been several months since I have shared food and fellowship with another believer. You sing?"

"Sing?" She took a scalding sip and thought of the many afternoons she spent sharing honey-sweetened tea with Mrs. Stern back in Yanji.

Mr. Tong rested his cup on the table and turned his head toward the window. "Sometimes I hear it, you know."

She followed his gaze. "Hear what?"

"Music. Sacred songs my grandmother taught me. She grew up with church. But that was before ... What did you say your name was?"

Hannah froze.

Mr. Tong sighed. "Forgive me. I should not have asked. But tell me, do you know any hymns?"

She rolled her tongue across her lip. "Yes, we were taught some at our ..." She took another sip of tea, glad that Mr. Tong could only hear her stammer and not also see her blush. "Yes, I know some hymns."

He leaned forward in his chair "You will sing for me, no?"

She lowered her cup. "Now?"

Mr. Tong had already closed his eyes and clasped his hands on the table. A serene, expectant smile spread across his face. Hannah glanced around the room nervously before she began. The old man's body swayed in time with the music.

"Sweetly, sweetly now I rest,
Joy and comfort, I am blessed.
Not a sorrow, not a fear,
While these loving words I hear."

She sang as quietly as possible. Mr. Tong's neighbors didn't live very close, but she couldn't stand the thought of putting the old man in further danger. When she finished, he leaned back in his chair. They sat for several minutes in silence.

"Beautiful," he finally breathed. For a moment, she wondered if he had forgotten she was still there, but then he faced her again. "You will let me send you off with provisions, no? You have a long journey ahead of you." He stood up. "Here." He handed her two small sacks already prepared. She opened her mouth to protest. "Ahhh," Mr. Tong exclaimed, holding up a finger. "You think this is too much, no? But remember, I am an old man. I cannot feast like I once could. But you, you both have a long journey ahead of you. You must accept these. I insist."

Hannah took the bags.

He reached out and placed his hand on her shoulder. "And now we will pray before you go, no?" Without any hesitation, he lifted his voice to heaven. She wondered if he spent his days like this, in constant communion with the Father.

When the old man's blessing ended, she thanked him for the visit, quietly set the two sacks of food back on the table, and left. She walked back to the woods as the sun was rising, and a peace rested in her spirit. By the time she reached her backpack, her eyelids were half shut. She found a small clearing well out of sight of the main trail, made a shelter under some bushes, and let her exhausted body drift off to sleep.

CHAPTER 3

She woke up far later than she planned. The shadows had moved to the other side of the woods. She was so thirsty it was hard to breathe without coughing. She thought about returning to Mr. Tong's. Her next destination was at least five kilometers away. She could use another cup of tea before she traveled any farther. Why hadn't she accepted at least one of the old man's sacks of provisions? Didn't Jesus himself teach his disciples to eat what was set before them?

It was still several hours before nightfall. If Mr. Tong's neighbors saw her visit, they might grow suspicious. On the other hand, it was a long way to her next delivery, and she didn't know if there would be any food to forage or any streams to drink from along the way. During the Great Hardship, the famine that ravaged Hannah's childhood, she would often go whole days without eating. But after spending a full year with the Sterns, she wasn't accustomed to the discomfort of hunger or the intensity of thirst.

Biting the inside of her cheek, she made up her mind. She couldn't put Mr. Tong in extra danger just for a little snack. If the Lord wanted her to make it to her next meeting, he would give her the strength to get there. She stood up and hefted her pack onto her back. As she began her slow hike through the woods, she regretted giving all the food away to the flower-swallows in Yanji. Wouldn't God understand if she kept a few granola bars for herself? Since she was doing the work of the Lord, she needed to keep up her energy so she could complete her tasks, didn't she?

She recalled one evening she spent with Simon in Mrs. Stern's garden discussing the Sermon on the Mount. "When Jesus says, *Ask, and you will receive,*" Hannah had questioned, "do you think that's a promise or just a generalization?"

Simon frowned. "A promise, I guess. Why do you ask?"

Hannah thought about the people who lived in her village during the Great Hardship, the believing mothers who prayed in vain for food every day, the hungry children who ended up abandoned on the streets once their parents starved. "It's just sometimes I wonder, you know? Like what about ..." She fumbled for the right words.

"The famine," he answered with a sigh. It was the only time he hadn't been able to answer one of her theological questions.

When Hannah had walked less than a kilometer from Mr. Tong's, she arrived at a small stream. Her first thought was what she'd tell Simon about what God did for her the first day of her mission. *A real answer to prayer. Just like Jesus said.* She took her backpack off, knelt down, and cupped the water to her mouth like the soldiers in Judges. She thought about the story of Gideon. Would she feel any braver if an angel spoke with her?

After she drank, she sat back against a tree. She loved the sound of the rippling stream. Compared to Yanji, everything here was so peaceful. There were no roads or homes or people in sight. Nothing but God, the river, the trees ...

Stretching her legs in front of her, she took off the paper around her neck and studied the map. She didn't have time to waste, but as soon as she stood up, she had to grasp the tree trunk to support herself. She was so hungry, the whole woods looked like it was spinning. She pressed her hand against her empty belly and chastised herself. After God answered her prayers and led her to water, was she now going to demand food as well? How was she any better than the Israelites who grumbled in the wilderness as soon as the Lord led them across the Red Sea?

She knelt down again by the stream. At least she could fill her stomach with water. She reached into her bag for the empty bottle and found three granola bars. How could she have missed them earlier? She was too famished to wonder for very long. Her mouth watered as she opened one of the wrappers with trembling fingers. She hadn't even been in North Korea for twenty-four hours, and already God had met every one of her needs. She thought back to last night in the woods, how scared she had been in the dark, and rebuked herself for acting so foolish. What would Simon think if he had seen her?

A branch snapped a few paces behind her. She spun her head around. There was nothing to be afraid of. Hadn't she memorized all those Bible verses about courage for a reason? She needed to take her thoughts captive instead of letting fear hold its powerful sway over her. What would the Sterns say? What would Simon say? She needed to move on. She took a bite of granola bar and then stood, swinging her backpack up to her shoulders.

"*Softly, softly in my ear, Jesus whispers, 'I am near.'*"

A few minutes later Hannah paused. The back of her neck tingled. Was that a twig breaking behind her? She felt her spine go rigid. *It's nothing,* she told herself. *Just a squirrel.* She strained her ears but only heard her own pulse. It was silly to be so fearful. Of course she wasn't alone. How many perfectly safe animals lived here and watched Hannah from their camouflaged homes? She wasted enough time last night. Courage or no courage, she needed to press on.

"*'It's my hand that guides your way, I'll protect you night and day.'*"

A bolt of color flashed in her periphery. She clenched the straps of her bag and didn't dare glance around. Her mind told her to run, but her body wouldn't respond. She held her breath and could only focus on one thought: *Somebody's here.* But who would be following her in the forest? It if were a North Korean agent, he would have stopped her by now, wouldn't he? Unless he was trailing her to find out who her next contact was.

A small breeze sent shivers scurrying up Hannah's spine. She thought of her crisis training. Hadn't Mr. Stern primed her for situations just like this? If she was lucky, it was just a hungry vagabond looking for someone to rob, but she had to assume her stalker came from the National Security Agency. She had to protect the believers whose names and addresses she carried around her neck. She was too small to fight off an attacker, agent or not.

She counted to five, keeping her movements slow and deliberate. Whoever it was out there, he couldn't know what she was about to do. With her back to her potential assailant, she crept her hand beneath her sweater and freed the list that hung from her neck. With her hand still concealed under her clothes, she crumbled the paper into a small, tight ball. She didn't hear any movement from behind, but she kept her body tense and ready for his assault. She fingered the crumpled list. It was small enough she probably wouldn't choke, but swallowing it wouldn't be easy. There was nothing else to do. She lifted her hand to her mouth slowly, hoping it looked as if she were just about to yawn or scratch her cheek.

"Stop!" Someone raced toward her from behind, crunching branches, trampling leaves. She shut her eyes, braced her body, and managed to shove the wadded paper into her mouth just as a hand clamped down over her face. The attacker grabbed her arms from behind. Her backpack dropped to the floor, and she bent over, gagging. The ball dropped from her mouth. She reached for it.

"Hannah, don't."

All the blood froze in her veins.

CHAPTER 4

Jai-Bong threw his hat on the driver's seat and dropped his coat down next to it. He strode up to the old man's door, which opened before he could knock. Mr. Tong's leathery face crinkled into a hundred wrinkled tributaries. "I heard your van as you pulled in. You are most welcome, Brother." He swung the door open wide. "Your visits are always most refreshing to me."

Jai-Bong returned the blind man's bow and followed him into the house, where he frowned at the obligatory portrait of the Dear Leader. "You are doing well?" he asked.

"Quite." Mr. Tong clasped Jai-Bong by his hands. "But I'm sorry, Brother. I only have plain tea to offer. I just gave a friend the rest of your ginseng this morning."

"No matter." Jai-Bong reached into his pocket and pulled out a small root. "You know I never come empty-handed."

He took the gift in his shaking hands. "The Lord always provides for us, no?" His head bobbled back and forth as he ambled to the counter.

Jai-Bong took a chair and stretched out his legs. "So you had visitors today?"

"Just one." Mr. Tong faced Jai-Bong. "And now two. The Lord has blessed me."

"Indeed." Jai-Bong studied the room. Two small sacks rested on the table. Nothing else had changed since his last visit.

Mr. Tong placed the kettle on the stove. "My first visitor brought me the greatest of gifts."

Jai-Bong leaned forward. "Did he, now? How providential. Bibles, then?" Jai-Bong squinted and studied the room once more.

"She was young. With the voice of the angels."

Jai-Bong frowned. "She?"

"Oh, yes." Mr. Tong reached for a knife.

Jai-Bong stood up to help.

"I thought she must have someone else with her. For safety, no? But she said she was quite by herself."

"Really?" Jai-Bong fingered his ring. "What was her name?"

"She was young. Not older than my beloved when we married." While the tea steeped, Mr. Tong prattled on, telling Jai-Bong about the Bibles he would deliver to the people in his village. "I wish I were vigorous enough to travel the entire province like before." The old man hung his head. "But at least some young ones now carry the work on for us, no?"

"It would be dangerous for a man in your condition to hike around North Hamyong with Bibles in your pockets."

"I know, Brother. I know. But I still would if I had the strength, understand. But the good Lord must know what he's doing. He allows me to serve him here, and he sends me company like you and ..."

"Me and who?" Jai-Bong leaned forward.

Mr. Tong paused until the gyrations in his torso slowed down a little. "She couldn't tell me. It's a shame, really. Most likely I'll never learn her true name until we meet in heaven."

Jai-Bong fingered his badge. "Yes. A shame." His head was racing with information, but the blind man kept prattling. When the tea was ready, they sat and drank, and Mr. Tong spilled more than he sipped. Jai-Bong waited as long as cultural etiquette demanded and then cleared his throat. "I fear it's time I should be going."

"Won't you sing a hymn with me first?" Mr. Tong clutched Jai-Bong's wrist.

Jai-Bong frowned and looked out at his van. "You know that would be dangerous."

"A prayer, then. Stay a moment, and I will pray over you, no?"

Jai-Bong scowled out the window. It would be dark by the time he got back to work. "Of course." He stooped his head.

"Our most gracious heavenly Father ..."

Jai-Bong stood up straight, his eyes opened wide, while the old man prayed. *A girl. Delivering Bibles.*

"How I praise you for my brother, who comes to refuel my weary spirit and blesses me with his fellowship."

Young. Traveling alone.

"I ask your protection and grace to go before him. Strengthen him for the work you've called him to. Encourage him for the tasks ahead of him."

Probably fresh from across the border. From that Secret Seminary in Yanji, maybe?

"Keep him safe from those who would try to harm him. Protect him from the eyes of the National Security Agency and the neighbors who might turn him in."

Who had sent her? And was she really by herself?

"Most of all, bless him with the presence of your Holy Spirit and sustain him until the day North Korea embraces the gospel or until you call him home."

Jai-Bong didn't linger. After a hasty "Amen," a few exchanged bows, and a promise to visit again soon, Jai-Bong shut the cabin door behind him. Safe in his van, the National Security agent punched a button on his handheld radio.

"This is General Sin. I'm coming in right now."

***

They had spent a year of their lives together at the Secret Seminary, but this was the first time Simon saw Hannah cry. He wrapped his arms around her, and she buried her face into his chest. "You scared me so much."

"I'm sorry. I ... I didn't really want you to find me. Not yet." Could she hear how fast his heart was racing?

"I am so glad to see you," she breathed.

"You have no idea how thankful I am to hear you say that."

She wiped her cheek. "What do you mean?"

"For as long as I've known you, I've never seen you break one rule. Not one." He pulled away. If he held her for even a minute longer, he would never find the strength to let her go again. He let his fingers brush against hers for a brief moment before dropping his hands to his sides. "You'll probably hate me for this, but I've been following you." She didn't say anything. Was she angry? He hurried to clarify. "It just didn't seem right, sending you out all alone. No one to look out for you. I know the Sterns said it was safer to travel separately, but, well, you're so young. And if anything happened to you, and I wasn't there to protect you ..."

She raised her eyes to meet his. "I understand." His throat burned. He reached for her hand, and this time her fingers intertwined with his.

He shifted his weight. "It just didn't seem right, walking away from you, always wondering what happened to you. I didn't think I'd be able to handle not knowing."

"Me, either."

He heard the tremor in her voice but resisted the urge to take her in his arms again. They had work to do. "I wasn't planning to scare you like that. I was hoping you wouldn't even notice me. Then, when I saw what you were about to do with that list ..." Simon laughed. "Did Mr. Stern teach that to you one day when I was sleeping in?"

Her expression was enough to cut off his chuckle. "How long were you going to keep following me?"

Simon stared at her bare toes. "Until I knew you were taken

care of, I guess. And I thought you might need some more granola bars." She scrunched up her face, so he explained. "I saw you give your food away to those kids at the bus station, and I ... well, honestly, I was ashamed. I wouldn't have even thought of that. And then it made me even more worried for you. I mean, here you are less than a day into ministry, and you've already given away your shoes and all your food." Her face fell. He placed both hands on her shoulders. "I didn't mean that in a bad way. Like I said, it made me ashamed of myself. But it also made me want to look out for you. Make sure you had everything you'd need."

"So those extra granola bars were from you?"

There wasn't any righteous way to deny it. "I put them in your backpack when you were making your first delivery."

"You've been with me this whole time?"

"From a distance, mostly. Sometimes closer than others."

"I thought I heard something last night."

"I never meant to scare you."

"What about your own assignment?"

He stared at a point just past her ear. "I'll still finish it. Soon."

She lowered her eyes. "Thank you for being with me. I was really hoping that ... I mean, I really needed some extra courage."

"So you're not upset?" Simon held his breath, studying every muscle, every pore, every blemish on her upturned face.

She smiled softly. "Even Jesus told the disciples to go out two by two, didn't he?"

He picked up her backpack and hefted it over his shoulder. In response to some silent agreement, they both set off at the same time, with Hannah ever so slightly in the front to lead the way to her next delivery.

***

She was panting by the time they stopped at dusk. Simon

lowered their backpacks and sat down near a grove of trees. "You get some rest," he said. "I'll keep watch."

She had napped almost the whole day away after her meeting with Mr. Tong. She wasn't sure she could sleep now even if she wanted to. She studied Simon's darkened face. "How much rest have you had since we left the Sterns'?"

"An hour or two. Not nearly as much as you." He grinned. Hannah stretched her legs and checked her map. They were about a kilometer or so from her next delivery site. The house was near the center of town, so they would have to wait several more hours until it was dark. There were worse ways to pass the time than sitting next to Simon, watching the massive clouds outlined in pink from the setting sun.

He rolled his neck from side to side. "I'm not sure I can sleep right now, either."

She felt her cheeks warm up. She brushed off some imaginary dirt from her pants. "Were you planning to come with me all along?"

He drummed his fingers against his knees. "Not in so many words."

She raised an eyebrow.

"I just knew I couldn't leave you alone," he explained. "But I never consciously decided to follow you. At first, I thought I'd just wait around and make sure you crossed the river all right. But when you gave away your shoes and all your food, I knew I couldn't let you go by yourself. I thought you might need me." He stared down at his chest and mumbled into his shirt collar, "Just like I need you."

The words were so quiet Hannah wondered if she heard them right. Or maybe she wasn't meant to hear anything at all. He looked up at her. "I don't want to do this alone." He took her hand in his. "I want to stay together. Help each other out." She didn't know what to say. He peered into her eyes. "Well?"

"Yes." Hannah didn't realize her lips were trembling until she tried to smile. "Yes. That's what I want, too."

CHAPTER 5

With trembling hands, Mr. Tong rinsed his teacups and placed them on the counter. He could not remember the last time he had been blessed with two visitors in one day. He thought about the young girl who brought him the New Testaments, his memories morphing seamlessly into prayer. "Such a young one. Pretty voice." Mr. Tong had lived alone ever since the Peninsula War. His wife and son had fled south ahead of him, but he did not make it out in time. He could not remember when he started speaking out loud. Sometimes he grew too careless; even conversations with the air could incriminate him if the wrong neighbor happened to overhear.

After drying the dishes, he walked over to the framed photograph of the Dear Leader. Years of loneliness taught him that even a portrait was better company than an empty house. Behind the picture frame hid a loose brick. Mr. Tong groped with his fingers and reached into the small opening. First, he pulled out one of the new audio devices. It was not safe to listen to now, but he fingered the buttons of the small machine, drinking in the ecstasy that coursed through his arm at the simple touch. He reached farther back and took out one of the New Testaments. He closed his eyes, a vestigial gesture from his seeing days, and brought the small book up to his nose. Inhaling deeply, he relished the scent of the thin paper, overwhelmed by an awe too deep to express in human language. He had never been blessed with much musical skill, but his silent praises floated heavenward to the throne room of God Almighty.

Mr. Tong swayed, the result of his rapture as much as his palsy. He would never be able to read again, not until his Savior called him up to heaven and gave him a new body, but he counted himself as one of the most blessed men in the world, for in his hands was the living and active Word of God.

***

His right arm is under my head and his left hand embraces me. The verse made Hannah blush. The Song of Solomon certainly wasn't one of the books the Secret Seminary members discussed together, but the Sterns encouraged the students to study Scripture independently. Hannah never made it through the entire Bible like Simon, but she stumbled across Song of Solomon one day and read all eight chapters in a single sitting. Afterwards, she was riddled with guilt for peering into such a romantic account of longing and passion, but she was too embarrassed to talk about it with Mrs. Stern. She certainly never mentioned it to Simon.

After that first instance, she decided she probably shouldn't look at the Song of Solomon again unless she ever got married, which was an unlikely event, given her calling. Still, that verse was all she could think about while she watched Simon sleep. Her whole body heated up with each rise and fall of his chest. She resisted the urge to sweep some of his dark hair off his brow. He looked so tender, his head resting on Hannah's backpack, his feet curled up behind him like a small child's. She could picture how snug she would fit if she were to curl up in front of him, the curve of his body perfectly matching hers.

She bit her lip and looked away. Should she have confessed her clandestine reading to Mrs. Stern? Maybe then the words wouldn't have such power over her. *If the Son has set you free, you shall be free indeed.* God would need to deliver Hannah from her unruly emotions. Perhaps it would have been better if Simon hadn't come with her after all. But she couldn't keep her eyes away from his peaceful slumber and realized she would do almost anything to keep him here beside her.

***

"You are not safe yet. Wait another few days." Mr. Tong had been arguing with himself for the past half hour. Since he no longer had an audio Scripture recording of his own, he was eager to hear the words of his Savior once more. He shook his head from side to side as he shuffled across the room. "You had two visitors today," he whispered. "You will be under suspicion. Wait it out, no? You will have your chance soon enough."

He groaned as he lowered himself onto his sleeping mat, remembering again to pray for the young girl who visited him earlier. "Heaven knows I cannot make the kind of journeys she does anymore." As usual, the mental image of his young bride smiled down on him as he worked to get comfortable in his bed. She would be an octogenarian by now if she were still alive, but he pictured her as she was when he last saw her, a young mother with twinkling eyes. "You know I miss you more every single day, no?"

He pulled his blanket up to his chin. The threadbare material did nothing to ward off the cold, but it served as a faint reminder of the way his beloved wife had curled up against him while they slept side by side so many years ago.

***

Hannah was thankful the darkness hid her flushed cheeks when Simon finally woke up.

"How long have I been asleep?"

"Two hours. Maybe three." She turned away, embarrassed to

hear how groggy his voice sounded. If he married one day, is that what his wife would hear every morning?

He looked up. "Cloudy."

She nodded. She had noticed, too. It would make it that much easier for them to stay hidden. Even though Simon was with her, she was more nervous about this delivery than she had been about Mr. Tong's. The address was in the middle of town, and they would have to walk past several houses before coming to the right one. "I don't know how long we have until morning," she observed. "We better get going."

"We?"

She bit her lip. She had assumed he would come with her. "You're right. I guess it's safer if I go alone." She opened up her backpack and took out two audio units.

"What are you doing?"

"Getting ready."

He placed his hand over hers. "I thought we agreed that this stuff is too dangerous for you."

At first, she was too surprised to protest. What was he saying? That he expected to take over all the work now they were together?

He fingered the string around her neck that held the crumpled piece of paper she had tried so hard to protect. "Here. You better give me your contact list, too."

She snatched it back. "No." She hadn't meant to sound that forceful. "I mean, this is my assignment. I ... I want to have a part in it."

Simon gently opened her fist. He took the contact list and stuffed it into his coat pocket, letting his fingers linger on hers. "You do have a part in it. We're working together, remember?" He opened the backpack a little wider and took out a few more audio players and New Testaments. "I'll be back soon."

"Are you sure you don't want me to come with you?" she

asked in a faint whisper.

He stood up, his body so close to hers he could have reached out and wrapped both arms around her if he chose to. "I don't want to worry about you. I couldn't bear it if something happened." A dozen arguments flashed through her mind. She hadn't risked her life to cross the border just to become someone's pack mule. She kept her mouth shut.

He brushed her cheek with his finger. "Promise me you'll stay safe."

She hoped he didn't notice her body tense. "I will." She wished he would hold her in his arms once more, like he had near the stream.

He zipped up his coat. "I'll be back soon."

"I'll be here."

***

"Get up, old man," the gruff voice demanded.

Mr. Tong did not open his eyes but counted three pairs of hands on him, dragging, yanking, tugging him out of bed.

"You are welcome here, strangers." He hoped his assailants knew his hands trembled with age, not with fear. "I will make you a cup of tea, no?"

"Shut up, dog."

Mr. Tong noted the crispness of their uniforms. National Security Agency. Decades of clandestine work for the underground church had finally caught up with him. He nodded his head, thankful this last pilgrimage of his was not taking place in the merciless chill of winter. His hole-ridden blanket fell forgotten to the floor.

"May you use my home as a sanctuary for others," he whispered before a guard elbowed him in the ribs. He did not cry out when they forced him out the door. He stumbled in the dark, and an agent shoved him into a car. He lifted his chin high. He would not be ashamed. He would not show them fear. He had survived the past five decades only guessing what happened to his wife.

If he died tonight, he would either be reunited with his beloved or at least be able to watch her from above.

CHAPTER 6

Hannah paced back and forth while she waited for Simon. Her footsteps on the crunching leaves made far too much noise, but she didn't care. If he planned to take over her entire mission, why had she sneaked back into North Korea at all? If he was just going to snatch all the Bibles and deliver them himself, why had she ever left the abundance and relative safety of the Sterns'? She should just give him her backpack and return to Yanji.

Did he doubt she could complete her assignment? Was that why he followed her? For the briefest moment, she wondered if Mr. or Mrs. Stern had asked him to look after her. She huffed and recalled the Sterns' incessant grilling over the past several months: *Are you certain you want to go back to North Korea? Are you sure you're ready? We could help you relocate to South Korea where you'll be safe.* Was it because she was a girl? Was that why nobody believed in her?

At first, she was grateful for Simon's company. Ecstatic, even. She had never agreed with the Sterns' decision to send them out alone. How were they supposed to endure without any fellowship or encouragement from one another? The graduates, not the Sterns, were the ones risking their lives sneaking into North Korea. The American missionaries had never set foot in Hannah and Simon's cut-off, isolated kingdom. What right did they have to tell the graduates how to travel? Simon's appearance in the woods had felt like divine providence, an answer to all her unspoken hopes.

For the first few hours.

And now he wouldn't even let her finish her tasks. *Her* tasks, the one the Sterns entrusted specifically to her. She leaned her head back and glared at the night sky. With the thick covering of clouds, she had no way to tell the time. She was supposed to make her way to the center of the village, leaving Bibles and audio devices for a Christian living there. She wasn't supposed to sit in the woods and count down the seconds. Simon had come to protect her, or so he claimed, but how was she any safer here than in the village itself? If the National Security Agency found her, they'd punish her no matter where she was caught.

She huffed when the first drops of rain splashed on her forehead. She was tired, alone, and completely unprotected. A few minutes later, she was also soaking wet.

***

"You had a visitor this morning. Who was she?" The interrogator leaned in so close Mr. Tong could smell the sour tinge of vinegar on his breath.

"I did not have the honor to learn her name." Mr. Tong was thankful he was blind. The interrogator, no matter how hard he might try, would never get a physical description out of him.

"I'll make you talk, old man. Whether your god saves you depends on how much information you give me." To make his point, he grabbed one of Mr. Tong's fingers and wedged a sharp needle into the soft spot between the nail and the flesh underneath. "What was her name?"

Mr. Tong tried to keep his head steady, but the palsy just traveled down to his free hand.

The interrogator laughed. "I'll make you quiver before the night's through, Christian pig. Now tell me who your visitor was."

Mr. Tong waited until his trembling subsided. Then he lifted his chin. "Even if I knew, I would never betray her to someone like you."

The interrogator snorted. Mr. Tong heard the sound of metal clinking against metal. "I had a feeling you'd say that."

***

Simon walked as fast as he dared. His only goal was to make the delivery and return to Hannah as soon as possible. He hated leaving her alone. Did she even know what dangers awaited her on this side of the Tumen River? Up until the day they graduated, he hoped she would back out of the program, but her heart was set on fulfilling this mission. He shouldn't have followed her, but he needed to know she was safe. At least now he could protect her, and he would keep on protecting her as long as he was breathing.

He hurried to the village with both hands clenched. Everything was as it should be. He would pass a hundred sleepless nights or cross a dozen flowing rivers if it kept Hannah cradled in the arm of safety. He recalled the feel of her head against his chest when she hugged him earlier today. When they found the grove of trees and he lay down to rest that afternoon, her physical closeness nearly drove him to distraction. It had taken him twice as long as it should have to fall asleep.

Even so, he knew his longings were nothing more than fantasy. Once North Korea was open to the gospel, once his compatriots were free to worship Christ publicly, he could consider the luxury of marriage. Until then, there was too much work to do. He wiped cool drops of rain off his cheeks and forced his senseless musings out of his mind. He had a delivery to make. It was time to focus. If anything went wrong, he had to be ready to run and get back to Hannah. With ears strained and muscles tense, he hurried on.

He was going so fast he didn't even notice the child crouched beside the trail. After nearly tripping, Simon caught his balance and spun around. The boy thrust a crumpled piece of paper into his palm, darted off, and disappeared. Simon scanned the note. *Don't go back the way you came. Unsafe. You will find shelter here.* A crude map marked a point on the opposite end of the village.

With his breath stuck somewhere between his throat and his lips, Simon turned back on the trail. His lungs bursting, he raced back through the woods toward Hannah. He had to get her out of there.

***

By the time she heard the men and calculated how fast she had to move to outrun them, Hannah's legs were frozen in place. A flashlight blinded her eyes. The men rushed closer. She bit her tongue to keep from crying out. She couldn't let Simon hear. He'd run to her rescue, and then they'd both be taken. The guards would reach her in just another second or two. She glanced up at the olive-green uniforms. National Security Agency. It was too late for her. One of the men grabbed a handful of her hair and pressed his lips against her ear. Nausea threatened to knock her off her feet as his coarse stubble scratched her skin.

"Going for a walk in the rain?"

The backpack was only a few paces away, but she refused to look at it. *Keep it hidden, Lord,* she prayed. When Simon came back and found her missing, at least he could take the Bibles to those who needed them.

For the first time since she left Yanji, the verses she memorized about fear flowed from her spirit without effort. *Have I not commanded you, be strong and courageous. Do not be terrified, do not be discouraged, for the Lord your God will be with you wherever you go.* God had sent Simon to walk with her for a day. Now the two of them would be torn apart once again, and the Holy Spirit himself would have to give Hannah the power and strength she needed to carry on.

The first agent clenched her hair, exposing her throat, and his partner walked in slow circles around her. "Look what we have here." Both men chuckled.

She focused all her energy on inhaling and exhaling. *Though an army besiege me, my heart will not fear. Though war break out against me, even then will I be confident.*

"It's not safe for a little girl to be out alone in the big, dark woods." He stopped and stroked her cheek. His finger ran down to her neck. "You never know what could happen to a nice little thing like you."

She thought about the backpack. If she could get them to leave now, it might stay hidden. "Where are you going to take me?" She tried to sound brave, but her voice was betrayed by an incriminating squeak.

The man frowned and shook his head. The other agent twisted her arm behind her back. Her heart pounded in her chest, its thud echoing loudly in her ears. She followed the men. She had to get them as far away from the backpack as possible. She prayed Simon wouldn't return until they were gone. She prayed he would find the Bibles where she left them.

The ministry had to continue.

CHAPTER 7

Simon doubled over. He whispered her name but knew she was gone. He waved the flashlight around the empty grove. Nothing. With a groan, he hurled the light to the ground and smashed the lens with the heel of his boot. Why Hannah? She was too young, too innocent. He hated thinking about what might befall her in enemy hands, but his mind would focus on nothing else. He wiped his nose on his sleeve and stumbled blindly into the woods.

He should have never left her alone. He failed her. He failed everybody. He shipwrecked his own mission and kept Hannah from carrying out hers as well. If he hadn't followed her around like a stricken mutt, she would still be safe. The warning message would have reached her in time to hide. What had possessed him to think they could travel safely together?

He stumbled blindly into the woods but couldn't guess which direction to turn. He was soaking wet from the rain. And even if his flashlight still worked, any tracks would be washed away by now.

He sank down against a tree trunk. "I'm sorry." He covered his head with his hands, swallowing away the painful lump in his throat. "I'm so sorry."

He should have listened to Mr. Stern. It was too dangerous for missionaries to travel together. Why had he ever thought he could keep Hannah safe? Now everything was lost. Hannah, the backpack ...

The backpack. His head jerked up. He was no good to Hannah, the Sterns, or the underground church as long as he stayed here whining like a schoolboy. The graduates expected hardship. They were prepared for danger. Hannah went through the same crisis training as he. She was young, but she was strong. Stronger, perhaps, than Simon gave her credit for. When all the other girls dropped out of the program, she remained, sometimes even putting the older students to shame with her passion for the Lord. She would have given up her life, and gladly too, to see those Bibles safely delivered.

The backpack. It didn't just have the Bibles but also the map. If the National Security Agency found it, dozens of Christians, not just Hannah, could die. But what if they didn't have it? Hannah was a smart girl. If she saw the attackers coming, wouldn't she try to hide it?

Energized by this small spark of hope, Simon hoisted himself to his feet. He couldn't sit around paralyzed while there still might be deliveries to make. He clenched his jaw shut. At least she had given him the contact list. He only had a vague idea where he was, but he would wander these woods all night if he had to. He would search for the bag until winter claimed the entire countryside, and then he would dig under every snowdrift to reclaim it. He lifted his chin, ignored the raindrops pummeling his face, and tried to retrace his steps. He would complete the mission. God help him, he couldn't afford to fail.

***

"I said I'd make you talk," the interrogator sneered.

Lying on his stomach, his bloody cheek against the cold floor, Mr. Tong absorbed the vibrations from each boot stride as the guard paced back and forth in front of him. He hung his mouth open so the blood would not pool so much in his throat. Through toothless gums he muttered, "My God will protect her."

TORN ASUNDER

"I wouldn't be so bold in my convictions if I were you. You know you led us right to her." The agent pressed one boot down on the center of Mr. Tong's back, compressing his lungs. Unable to shift his weight, Mr. Tong let his breaths grow even shallower. He would not fight death. Why should he? He wondered if his beloved would look even more beautiful in heaven than he remembered her on their wedding day.

The weight lifted from Mr. Tong's back before he could pass out. What more did they want from him? "You'd better get some rest," the guard snarled. Mr. Tong had already lost feeling in his legs. He wished he could say the same about his arms. The guard spat on his cheek. "We'll have the girl brought in as soon as she arrives. You should save your strength. Watching us work when she gets here might make you ... tired, to say the least."

Still bound, Mr. Tong was unable to wipe away the tears that streaked down his bloody cheeks.

***

Do not be afraid of those who kill the body but cannot kill the soul. Tied and gagged in the backseat of a National Security van, Hannah tried to recall every lesson Mr. Stern taught her in crisis training. *"Chances are at some point you will be questioned. Admit to crossing the border if necessary, but don't let them know you've had contact with foreigners."* Hannah couldn't do it. These men were trained interrogators. How could she stand up to them?

She shut her eyes and pictured Mr. Stern standing behind her, whispering in her ear. *"They'll have ways to make you talk. Make up names. Give them false leads. Don't betray the other graduates or the Christians you've already met. You may not be able to save yourself, but at least the ministry will continue."*

Back in Yanji, Hannah had wondered if it would ever really

come down to that. Now she knew. *At least the ministry will continue* ... The men hadn't found the backpack. There were still reasons to rejoice.

By the time the van pulled up in front of the Chongjin jail, her trembling had subsided just a little, and she could breathe more smoothly. She didn't resist when her captors yanked her out of the car. She would be strong. For Simon's sake, she would endure.

***

"We got the girl. She's on her way here now."

General Sin gave a curt nod, ignoring the blood stains on Byung-Jun's shirt sleeve. "Very good." He marched down the hall, but then he stopped and spun around. "Kill the blind man. We don't need him anymore."

Byung-Jun shuffled his feet. "I thought I might keep him around while we talked with her."

"As you wish." General Sin dismissed the guard with a wave of his hand. So they found the missionary girl. He rubbed his chin. No surprises there. Still, the idea of foreigners sending a teenager over the border all by herself was a little incredulous. Did she have an accomplice, then? And when would this mysterious partner make an appearance?

It was time to pay blind Mr. Tong one last visit. He strode into the interrogation room, swinging the door wide open in front of him. The old man was splayed out in a puddle of blood. One leg bent behind him at an impossible angle. The only indication of life was the short, irregular tugging from his ribcage. He looked like a fish out of water just before it dies, still alive but no longer flapping around so pathetically.

Sin closed his eyes for a moment, and the smell of ginseng mingled with the dark stench of blood and mold that permeated the room. He stooped down to examine the man's mouth. Mr.

Tong wouldn't be answering any more questions. It was a pity. He would have liked more information before she arrived.

He stared at the body for a moment and allowed himself a heavy sigh. He turned on his heel when the old man muttered something. Sin scarcely made out the word. "Jai-Bong?"

He didn't answer. Instead, he took out his gun and aimed it at the back of the blind man's head. "Farewell, Brother," he whispered before pulling the trigger.

***

Hannah was still retching an hour after the agents threw her in the cell with Mr. Tong's butchered corpse. She hugged her arms around her stomach and heaved again.

"Seems your friend thought he could keep secrets from us." At first, the agent held Hannah's head in place with iron strength so she couldn't turn away. "He didn't want to tell us where you were going, you know. But eventually he found his tongue. And we found you."

She was too stunned to cry for the old man. There were still people alive she had to protect. The agents hadn't found the backpack. The list of contacts was safe. Simon was still free. She shouldn't have argued with him about staying behind in the woods. Now, at least he would be able to carry on the ministry without her. She had to be strong. No matter what they asked, no matter what they did, she needed to protect him and the believers on that list.

Hannah cowered on the floor in the cell, twisting away from Mr. Tong's mangled body. There was nowhere to look. Even when she closed her eyes, she saw his pale face, his bloody mouth, the sticky red hole in the back of his skull. She tried to recall a hymn, but singing praise in the face of such gore seemed almost blasphemous.

A guard opened the door, and Hannah wasn't sure if she

should shrink back or try to fight him off. He was tall, his cap perched high on his head. He was older than the other guards, but he didn't appear to have lost any strength or vigor. "I am General Sin." He yanked Hannah forward by the elbow. "You will come with me."

When Hannah was back in the Secret Seminary, she sometimes imagined how she would react if she were captured. She envisioned herself calm and serene, the Holy Spirit enveloping her in a beautiful quilt of peace and protection. General Sin pulled her so fast down the hallway she didn't have time to think or feel anything. She didn't even realize her lip was bloody where she bit it until he strapped her down in a chair in a cold, austere room. He clasped his hands behind his back, a mocking grin on his face. She glanced over her shoulder and recognized one of the agents who had captured her in the woods. He stood near a shelf, sorting through a gleaming metal toolbox.

"You will tell us who you are working with." General Sin leaned closer. His breath smelled like cigarette ash. "You will tell us where to find them. Or you will end up worse off than your blind friend."

Her mind was too paralyzed to process the threat.

"Who were you meeting tonight?" He dangled a pair of handcuffs in front of her face. "Give me the name of your contact."

The Sterns had warned her about these interrogations. Just the role-play scenarios from training gave Hannah nightmares for months.

General Sin cuffed her wrists to the chair. "You won't talk? Well, we'll see how you feel after Byung-Jun finishes with you." The younger guard pulled out a metal clamp that glistened in the light. She tried to clench her jaw. General Sin shrugged. "Of course, we could do this the easy way. Tell me what you know, and I'll transfer you to a more comfortable room."

She shook her head and squeezed her eyes shut. She couldn't

put Simon or the other Christians in danger. No matter what.

***

General Sin clenched his cigarette with his teeth while he watched the prisoner through a one-way mirror. Byung-Jun slipped in and shut the door.

"She's not breaking with orange. I'll move her up to green after this break."

General Sin raised an eyebrow. "She's just a child, Comrade. A little girl. And you're talking about green?"

"She must have been trained, sir." Byung-Jun's eye twitched.

"Trained by pathetic imperial missionaries," Sin spat. "And what about you, Comrade? Weren't you trained to gather information from underage Western spies?" He glared at the girl. She sat with her back to the wall, hanging her head. Part of him was glad his agent hadn't succeeded with her yet.

Byung-Jun bowed his head. "If we move her to green ..."

"Unacceptable." Sin spun away from the window. "You will keep her at orange, and you will make her talk. Unless you want everyone knowing a little girl got the best of you." He let the last comment linger in the air like a question.

Byung-Jun bowed again. "It will be as you say, sir."

General Sin whipped his head back to the mirror. "It better."

***

It was nearly dawn when Simon finally stumbled upon the alcove where he had left Hannah. How could he have failed her like this? He gritted his teeth. Did he really want to find the backpack? If Hannah was in custody, the guards would interrogate her. They'd demand to know why she was going from house to house and village to village. Once they learned about her mission and realized she left her contraband behind, they'd make her tell them where it was. She wasn't ready to stand up to their methods. Why had he left her alone? When his candlelight landed on the dark blue canvas of the hidden backpack, he wasn't sure if he should rejoice or not. Her interrogators would torture her until she told them where it was. If he took the bag now and the National Security Agency didn't find it where she said it was, what would happen to her then?

He swallowed down the growl rising up from his gut. How could he have failed her so miserably? He thought about leaving the backpack there so the National Security Agency would find it. But then what? It would only give them more evidence to convict her. Clenching his jaw, he heard Mr. Stern's warnings in his mind: *"The National Security agents will prey on your compassion for others. Don't give them that opportunity."*

Simon kicked the backpack, but his memories kept replaying Mr. Stern's admonitions. *"That's why you're safer going out alone. As harsh as it may sound, you need to focus on your mission, not on your comrades."* That was easy for him to say sitting on his American passport on the other side of the border. Still, Simon knew his mentor was right. If he didn't take the backpack, all the Bibles would be lost. Hannah's suffering would be for nothing. Nothing at all.

"I've always thought it would be a beautiful privilege to die for the sake of the gospel," Hannah had breathed one night while they sat side by side in the garden. He remembered the stately look in her eyes, and Simon knew what he had to do. The bag was heavy as he swung it onto his shoulder.

"Father, please protect her," he whispered and ventured out into the night.

PART 2

CHAPTER 8

"You say your partner was captured?" The man's eyes darted back and forth.

Simon nodded but kept his gaze to the floor. "Two weeks ago now. I came to warn you."

"Warn me?"

He lowered his voice. "You were one of the names on her list."

"I was on a *list*?"

"I have it here." Simon patted his pocket. "You were going to be her last delivery. I only thought it fair to tell you." He unzipped his backpack.

"What are you doing?"

"They didn't find our Bibles. I still have some for you."

The man took a step back. "You couldn't pay me to touch those."

Simon reached into the bag. "I could just leave you a few ..."

He shoved the backpack against Simon's chest. "Take your books and your list and get as far away from me as possible."

Simon hung his head. "If that's what you want."

"And don't ever dare contact me again."

Simon left the dilapidated cabin, trying to fight his feelings of dejection that weighed heavier than his half-full pack. Would he have accepted such dangerous materials under the same circumstances? All of the Christians he met with in the past two weeks were concerned, to say the very least, when he told them about Hannah's arrest. A few others refused the Bibles, though none with that same degree of vehemence.

He had hurried to meet her contacts as fast as he could, sometimes venturing forth in broad daylight to save time. The National Security agents would do everything to coerce Hannah to remember every detail of her mission, and he wanted to be several steps ahead of the guards when they went out to investigate. If Hannah was alive, she would talk. That was just the way the agency worked. As long as she was in custody, he was in constant danger. The fact he was alive and free was unsettling. Was Hannah still alive? Then why hadn't they caught him yet? Was there anybody left for them to interrogate? He wasn't even sure how to pray for her. Should he trust in God for her miraculous release? And if she was already dead, would his prayers make any difference whatsoever?

Shouldering the backpack, he headed out from the village. There was nothing left for him here. He couldn't blame the man for refusing the Bibles, but did he have to be so rude? He thought about Mr. Stern's old saying: *"Never judge someone who fails a test you yourself have yet to pass."* Simon was keenly aware of his own shortcomings. He had neglected his entire mission so far and had focused only on Hannah's. He knew the Sterns would be disappointed.

He had contacted everyone on the list. Hannah's mission was complete. Now it was time for him to focus on his own assignment. He thought of the kilometers ahead of him, the sleepless nights traveling, the chilly days hiding. His limbs were heavy as he trudged on. Why hadn't the National Security Agency found him yet? Surely Hannah had told them everything by now. If she were still alive, at least.

An owl flapped overhead. Simon thought about his words with Mr. Stern just a few weeks ago. It was the closest Simon ever came to contradicting his mentor. "I still think it might be a better idea to send us out in pairs, even in spite of the risks."

Mr. Stern rubbed the hairless spot on the back of his head. "I know you want to stay with her, but I still say it's too dangerous."

Simon had blushed when Mr. Stern read his thoughts so clearly. "She's so young," he protested.

"And you're obviously in love and not fit to make rational decisions." The comment was meant in good humor, Simon was sure, but it pricked at him. Did Mr. Stern know what it was like to love somebody who was more likely to die from a firing squad than from sickness or old age? Did he know what it was like to be forbidden from staying with her as she marched off to her doom?

He stared at his benefactor. "Maybe I'll just marry her. Then you'll have to send us out together."

Mr. Stern reached out his hand. It pressed down heavily on Simon's shoulder. "If you were married, just think how easy it would be for the National Security Agency to get you to talk if you were captured. All they'd have to do is put a knife to your wife's throat ..."

"All right. I get it." Simon held up his hand. "You made your point clear enough."

Mr. Stern's sigh was strong enough to flutter the pages of the Bible on his lap. "I know you love her. But if you're both committed to going back to North Korea, well ... Trust me here, son. It could never work."

Weeks later, the pronouncement sat heavy on Simon's chest. *Never work.* Even though he loved her. And she loved him, he knew. *Never work.* It didn't seem right that this American missionary, this man of God, the one who had baptized them both, would have such little faith. Or did he just have more logic and reason? After all, Simon had tried to be with her. He hadn't kept her safe and only succeeded in proving Mr. Stern right.

He heard a noise and instinctively reached for the backpack. He chided himself for daydreaming. Why wasn't he paying better attention? He paused for only a second before he saw the flash of movement in the distance. He darted forward even before his mind fully registered the danger. His boots trampled on branches and dried leaves, and it must have been an act of God that he avoided tripping on any roots. He just had time to brace himself before someone plowed into him from behind. They both fell to the ground. Simon swung toward the man's nose. The attacker elbowed Simon's sternum, stealing his breath. The struggle was over in a matter of seconds. The olive-green cap was askew as his assailant stared down at him and raised the butt of his revolver. Simon knew he was doomed. Before he was knocked out, his one thought was that at least he had finished Hannah's mission for her. Maybe his life wasn't a total failure after all.

***

Hannah couldn't remember how much time had passed since her arrest. A month? More? Every few days, the guard would drag her to the interrogation room and barrage her with questions about her mission and her partners. She had to assume Simon was still free or the men wouldn't be asking. Besides, the alternatives were too horrific. *"There are no good-byes in the kingdom of heaven,"* she had whispered to him before they both left Yanji. She wanted to laugh at herself. How little she had known back then.

She still hadn't told the agents about Simon or the other Christians she was supposed to contact. One leg was rendered completely useless. The worst part wasn't the pain, but the complete isolation. They kept her locked in darkness for days with no reprieve or human contact whatsoever. She spent all her mental and spiritual stamina wrestling with the temptation to tell her captors everything just so she could see light again.

Twice a day or so, someone passed a bowl of tasteless gruel into her cage, but there were no toilets or sinks, no bed to lie down on or chairs to sit in. The ceiling was too low for Hannah to stand up, and her back ached for the chance to stretch. At some point during her incarceration, she started shivering. She hugged herself and rubbed her arms until she chaffed the skin. Nothing warded off the chills. Within a few more days, her throat was so swollen she couldn't swallow a single bite. Was this how she was going to die? Alone and forgotten in a windowless cell?

She slept fitfully, waking up to phantom sounds of iron doors and metal chains. Strange voices whispered in her dreams, calling her name, reaching out to her in the darkness.

"Hannah?"

The sound came from only a few feet away, right in the cell. Was she delirious, then? Was the fever that bad?

"Hannah?"

She froze. She knew that voice. It couldn't be. "Brother Simon?" she croaked. "Is that you?"

CHAPTER 9

She wanted to rush to him, but both her ankles were chained to the wall. She coughed once. If her heart sped up any faster, she might pass out. "Is it really you? Are you hurt? How long has it been? A month?"

"Two weeks," he mumbled. She could hardly hear him.

"I didn't think I'd ever see you again."

"Please ... Don't." His voice was weak. What had the agents already done to him?

Hannah wanted to tell Simon how much she had missed him. She wanted him to know how often she had prayed for him. She thought back to the Bible story when Paul and Silas were imprisoned together for preaching the gospel. They sang praises all night long. She would give almost anything to hear Simon's off-key voice fumbling through a few verses of *Amazing Grace*. "I'm sorry they caught you, too." She recognized the pleading in her own voice and wondered what Simon was thinking. "Did you finish the deliveries?" she asked. "Did you ..."

"Shut up," he growled. "Don't you know they're listening?"

She lowered her head. Of course the guards would eavesdrop. She shouldn't have mentioned the Bibles. But couldn't they talk about other things? Maybe if they comforted one another, they could show the guards they weren't afraid. Maybe if he talked to her, she would stop feeling so scared. She could reach her fingers just far enough to caress the back of his hand, but he jerked it away. "I just wanted ..." she tried to explain.

"Stop."

Why was he angry at her? What had she done? He didn't blame her for getting caught, did he? She thought about everything that had happened since her arrest, how much she had agonized over his safety. The only reason she didn't give in to her interrogators was to guarantee he stayed safe. No matter what they asked, no matter what they did, she had refused to tell them where he was. But they found him anyway. And now he was furious at her.

She took a deep breath. Did he think it was her fault? She swallowed once. "I didn't tell them, you know." He was silent. Was there any way she could lift his spirits? Wasn't that why they had decided to travel together in the first place — to be an encouragement to one another? "I never betrayed you." Uneasiness sat in her stomach like a rock. Tentatively, she reached out in the darkness until she found his shoulder.

His whole body heaved with silent sobs.

***

General Sin frowned as he sat listening in the surveillance area. His lip twitched slightly. With fumbling hands, he lit a cigarette and listened while the new prisoner chided the girl for talking about their so-called "secret" mission. So, the boy had more brains than courage. General Sin flicked his cigarette to the ground and punched the screen off. He had heard enough.

***

Simon would have shaken Hannah if they both weren't bound. There was nothing he could do to make her understand how it eviscerated him to have her so near, bound by chains just out of reach. She went on asking questions, apologizing, assuring him she hadn't given him away. She was clueless.

"Is that why you're mad?" she pressed. "Did you think I told them where you were?" Simon couldn't even imagine what torture she had already endured the past two weeks while he roamed freely across the countryside.

He wished she would shut up. He had never let anyone watch him cry. Not even when he was a boy dying of starvation in the days of the Great Hardship. Why did they have to be chained in the same cell? Why did she have to see him like this?

"Please believe me." Hannah sounded as if she were close to tears herself. Simon felt like screaming. "I didn't tell them anything," she repeated.

He jerked his head up. "And why not?" He heard her gasp, but that didn't stop him from continuing. "All you had to do was talk. Give them my name. My location. My mission. Anything. Why didn't you tell them what they wanted to know?" He was sobbing again. He didn't care. They were both doomed. What did it matter if she saw his tears? What did it matter if she heard him shout? They had no future together except one of torture and death. "You should have told them anything. Everything. Why did you let them do this to you?"

The cell door jerked open. Someone released his handcuffs from the wall and yanked him to his feet.

"I was trying to protect you." Her voice was fragile. "You know why, don't you?" In the light from the hallway, he saw her glance up at him. In some other place, that single look would have filled him with unspeakable joy.

He lowered his head and followed after the guard. "That wasn't your job," Simon muttered to the floor.

The agent prodded him to the interrogation room. He was only a few centimeters taller than Simon, but he loomed over him with a menacing glare. "Name," he demanded as he strapped Simon to the chair. Spit landed on Simon's face. He had no more will to fight. He had already failed. Hannah suffered because of him. He let her down, and then he acted like a barbarian. Now both of them were going to die. At least he didn't have to play at heroics anymore. Simon gave his legal name.

"Who is the girl with you?"

"She goes by Hannah. I don't know her birth name."

"When did you meet her?"

"A little over a year ago." He wondered how much Hannah already endured on his account. She could have stopped it if she had just turned him in. His palms were sweaty, but the rest of his body shivered with cold.

"Is she your wife?"

He set his jaw. "No."

The young interrogator made a sound in the back of his throat. "That's a shame. She's quite ... alluring."

Simon lunged, but the chains cut into his wrists and held him fast. The guard chuckled and then resumed his questioning. "Have you ever been across the border?"

"No."

He raised an eyebrow. "Really? That's not what your lover told me."

Simon's body tensed, his muscles strained to break free from his bonds. He gritted his teeth. "She's not ... We don't ..."

The agent walked over to a shelf and opened a small case. "You say you've never crossed the border?"

Simon looked down into his lap. "No."

The man frowned, and a small silver scalpel glistened in his hand. "Unfortunately, I'm not quite sure I believe you."

What followed could have taken five minutes or two hours. All Simon knew was his throat was raw, and his ears rang with the echoes of his own screams. The guard was preparing some sort of needle when an older agent strode into the room. Simon couldn't focus on his features, but he saw his arms swaying as he walked. "Did you get a confession?"

"Well, no, Comrade General, but …"

The general cleared his throat.

"He gave us the name of a few towns," the guard squeaked. Simon struggled to remain conscious. What were they talking about? Was Hannah all right?

"You're dismissed." The general brushed the interrogator aside and studied Simon. "It hasn't been a good night for you," he remarked. Simon scarcely blinked. If they were busy breaking him down, that meant they weren't tormenting Hannah. The general laid his hand on Simon's shoulder. "I gather you didn't enjoy your conversation with my assistant. I assure you that my style is much more … refined, shall we say?" He wiped the bit of blood dribbling down from Simon's mouth with a rag. "Nothing to say? No matter. We'll have you talking before long."

He strolled over to the shelf of tools. "I'm sorry your little friend will have to see this." Simon felt his eyes widen. "You want to show her how brave you are, don't you?" He let one corner of his mouth curl up. "Of course you do."

The general took his radio out of his pocket. "I'm ready. Bring the girl in."

***

Hannah slumped against the wall and bit the inside of her cheek. Why was Simon so angry? What had she done wrong? She endured countless days in solitary confinement and merciless interrogations just to protect him. She had imagined how proud he would be if he ever found out. How thankful. He wouldn't consider her a child anymore, someone he had to look out for and protect. He'd understand she chose to suffer rather than risk his well-being. And somehow, if he had the courage to recognize it, he would know it was because she loved him.

She wiped her cheeks. Tears were a waste of energy here. Her body couldn't afford to lose the water. She needed to calm down before Simon returned. He couldn't see her like this. Her head was spinning, but she didn't know if that was a result of the illness or her anxieties. How much easier would life be if she had never met him?

The door clanged open. "Let's go." Rough hands unchained her from the wall. "Follow me." Her leg hung limp behind her, and she tried to hop to keep from being dragged down the entire hallway.

The guard nodded to his superior and left her in the interrogation room. Simon was already strapped into a chair, blood pooled near his mouth. "Hannah." The word was barely audible through his swollen lips.

"Welcome, my dear." The officer feigned a bow. "I can't offer you a chair, I'm afraid." He waved his wrist toward Simon. "Normally, I would ask the gentleman to relinquish his seat, but I'm not sure how willingly your friend would comply." Simon's back tensed, but he didn't say anything. General Sin's boots stomped on the floor, and Hannah felt each vibration through the concrete. He gave her a curt nod. "I brought you in for a very specific reason. It seems that you two know each other. Quite well, if I can trust my own judgment. But your friend here — Simon, I think you call him — is almost as stubborn as you, my dear." Hannah glanced at the chair where Simon glowered at them both.

"I'd like to make this easy for all of us." General Sin glanced alternately between her and Simon. "So let's start at the beginning, shall we?" She kept her eyes on his boots. "You." General Sin pointed at Hannah. "Who are you?"

She whispered her birth name. General Sin smiled. "Excellent. You see how easy this is? Do you prefer I call you Hannah? Why did you change it, by the way?"

She almost lifted her eyes to Simon, but she was afraid her look might betray more than she intended. "I took on a new name when I became a Christian."

"When you became a Christian." General Sin clasped his hands behind his back and nodded in mock understanding. "That's right. And this Simon friend of yours, he's a Christian too?"

Simon's chin tilted up slightly in what Hannah guessed was a nod. "Yes," she answered.

"Two Christians." General Sin smacked his lips together. "No papers. No work orders. Foreign boots," he added, staring at Simon's shoes. "And I'm supposed to believe you've both been minding your own business and keeping the peace?"

Hannah tried to keep her voice steady. "That's right."

General Sin turned to Simon. "And you'll corroborate her story, no doubt?"

"Every word."

Sin took a knife out of the box. "And what about you, Comrade Simon?" He made a show of testing the blade with his own thumb. Simon grimaced when it drew blood. "Do you want to explain to me what you were doing when my agents found you?"

"I was looking for work."

"I see." General Sin stopped in front of the tool box, making a show of selecting another metal object. "And how was it you managed to travel so far without proper papers?"

Hannah didn't realize she was holding her breath until she started to feel faint. Simon set his brow. "I was hungry."

"And that explains why we found you with foreign boots?" General Sin frowned at a long, metal needle. The point glistened in the electric light overhead.

"Just like I told the other guard, I found the boots near the train station. I thought they might be worth money, so I picked them up."

The general feigned a gasp. "Are you admitting you planned to sell stolen goods on the black market?"

Simon shrugged. "Who doesn't?" Hannah watched him in

amazement. She would have never guessed a Christian could lie so easily.

General Sin's smile vanished. "Who doesn't, indeed?"

***

Simon watched warily as General Sin set down the needle. "I see we're not getting very far here." He clucked his tongue. Anger surged through Simon, and he felt the veins in his neck throb. General Sin strutted over to the table of instruments. "Let's try things from a different angle, shall we?" He held up a small metal contraption for Simon to inspect. "We call this the junior guillotine. It's modeled after a French invention our Dear Leader is especially fond of. Would you like to see how it works?" He squeezed the device to demonstrate the swift slicing motion and then breathed in Simon's ear, "Careful, now. You wouldn't want to slip your finger in there by mistake."

Simon gritted his teeth. His head felt like it was sinking. The general kept his voice level and pleasant as he slipped the device over Simon's pinky. "Now, you just tell me who you delivered your Bibles to, and I'll let you leave here with everything intact."

Simon tried to swallow. His whole jaw was swollen from his scuffle in the woods. He shut his eyes and hoped the general couldn't feel him tremble.

General Sin chuckled to himself. "Silly me. I forgot." He slid the device off Simon's finger. "This kind of tool won't work on a big, strong man like you." He strode over to Hannah and yanked her hand before Simon could even cry out. He jammed her ring finger into the opening.

Simon struggled against his iron restraints. "Let her go!"

General Sin still glared at Simon. "This is your last chance. Give me the names, and I'll release her unharmed."

Simon's field of vision blurred over. He wanted to scream. The metal from his handcuffs sliced open his wrists. He envisioned himself breaking free and tackling the general to the ground.

"Better talk." General Sin yawned. "I have a meeting soon and really need to hurry things up."

Hannah's hand trembled, but she didn't make a noise.

"Three ..."

Simon clenched his jaw, unable to tear his face away from Hannah's wide, terrified eyes.

"Two ..."

"Stop!" He tried to leap out of his chair. "I'll do it!" His shout echoed against the whitewashed walls.

General Sin kept his eyes on Hannah but smiled. "I'm listening."

Simon rattled off as many names as he could remember, hardly pausing for breath. General Sin slipped the junior guillotine off Hannah's finger. She met Simon's gaze with a look that made his heart capsize.

General Sin helped her to her feet, and Simon almost detected a certain amount of chivalry in his touch. "You can go," the agent whispered and then barked into his radio, "Get the girl out of here."

Simon pulled once more against his restraints. *Don't let them hurt her*, he begged. Would he ever see her again? Did she know how much he ... Simon called out her name. She faced him, but when he saw her expression, he couldn't speak. Her eyes were filled with intense sorrow.

Sorrow and unmistakable pity.

CHAPTER 10

Hannah huddled in the corner of her cell. She wrapped her arms around her good leg and shivered. Two weeks. Two weeks of cruel interrogations, sleepless nights, endless confinement in the dark, moldy cell. Her throat was parched. She couldn't remember the last time they gave her any water. She hadn't stopped shivering in days. Two weeks of torture, two weeks trying to protect Simon and the Christians on her list. Two weeks of pain and torment, just so Simon could tell them everything within his first hour of capture.

She leaned her forehead against her knee. The room spun around relentlessly. She wanted to lie down, but the cage was too small. There were no tears to wash away this kind of pain, no prayers to cover over this kind of betrayal.

She lifted her head at the sound of footsteps. The agents would all expect her to cooperate now. And why shouldn't she? The Christian contacts were already exposed. Simon had made sure of that. He remembered even more names than she had, and he gave them all to the general one after another like relentless lashes from a whip. There was no more reason for her to protect any of them now. She didn't resist when the general ordered her to stand. She shuffled down the hall once more, ready this time to tell them anything they wanted to know.

General Sin led her to the interrogation room and sat her in the same chair Simon occupied just a little earlier. "I told you we'd get the information we needed." He didn't strap her in. "I'm sorry you had to witness your friend's ... weakness."

She clenched her jaw shut. He couldn't goad her.

When he brought his face close to hers, she cringed and tried not to breathe in the cigarette stink on his breath. "Perhaps if you weren't so pretty, your friend wouldn't have made such a fool of himself."

She shut her eyes, but that didn't block out his words.

General Sin clicked his tongue. "I admire you." He placed his hand on her shoulder, and she recoiled at his touch. "You're very brave." He eyed her up and down. "For a girl." She stared at the stained wall. "You won't accept my compliment, is that it?" He chuckled. "No wonder. I wouldn't either if I were you. But things are not always what they seem." He raised an eyebrow and then punched a button on his radio. "The prisoner is ready for transport."

Another guard sneaked in meekly. She hadn't seen him here before. He looked nearly as young as she.

"You will go with Agent Soon," General Sin told her and flicked a cigarette butt onto the floor.

Soon bowed to General Sin and kept his eyes downcast as he propped her up by the arm and helped her slide out of the chair. She glanced around the room, trying to gain some balance. Would she ever see Simon again?

She wouldn't have guessed how late it was until she saw the full moon setting on the horizon once Soon led her outside. A breeze flitted underneath the shirt of her prison uniform. She shivered and clutched her arms around herself.

"Get in." Soon prodded her with just enough force to guide her toward the van. She struggled with her weak leg, and he wrapped his arm around her waist. "Let me help you."

General Sin stood several paces away, glaring. "Hurry up."

All Hannah wanted was to rest. Soon eased her into the front seat of the van, circled around, and sat next to her behind the driver's wheel. His face was tight, but he relaxed almost as soon as they rolled away from the prison compound.

She swallowed, her throat still burning. "Where are you taking me?"

He didn't reply right away. He rubbed his chin and glanced around warily. Instinctively, Hannah did the same. "Shut up, prisoner," he barked and then cringed as soon as the words left his mouth. "No more talking. "

She was too tired to worry about his behavior. The van's bumping and swerving made her sick to her stomach, and it took all her effort to keep from throwing up. Her mind was foggy, and she leaned against the door, unable to sit up straight anymore. She rubbed her legs to try to create some extra warmth. Soon reached down and turned on the heater.

With her head bouncing against the van's window, she drifted in and out of consciousness. Every once in a while, she imagined she heard Simon singing. She wanted to tell him he was off-key, but she always jerked awake before she could say anything. She didn't know how long they traveled before Soon parked the van alongside a river. Hannah begged her body for the extra energy she would need to endure whatever was to come.

Soon got out of the van and crept over to Hannah's side. He opened her door and cleared his throat. "Get out, pig." He gently propped Hannah up in her seat, placing one hand on her forehead with a frown. She shivered in response. He reached around to lift her up and set her carefully on the ground.

"On your feet, lazy sloth!" He kept his arm around her, supporting nearly all her weight. "Now get moving." His voice was gruff, but his touch gentle. There wasn't enough light for Hannah to make out his features, and fear and confusion warred against each other in her gut.

Her throat stung, and her muscles quivered involuntarily, but she obeyed without question. She had survived two weeks in the Chongjin jail; she could endure this. They walked a few paces, Hannah doing what she could to drag her broken leg behind her and Soon nearly carrying her. When they came to a large tree stump, he eased her down on top of it. He felt her forehead once again before straining his neck in both directions. It took all of Hannah's concentration to keep her balance and not fall off.

He checked his watch. Sighing heavily, he reached down for a stick. He held up his empty hand toward Hannah, but she couldn't guess what his gesture meant to convey. Before she could react, he whacked the stump just centimeters away from her broken leg. Her faint cry hurt her throat, and she winced. Soon held her gaze and nodded.

"What are you doing?" she asked.

He held his finger to his lips and then tore off his coat and threw it on the ground.

Hannah tried to shrink back without falling. "Please ... don't," she croaked as he fumbled with his shirt buttons.

"Come on." His fingers dug into her skin. She couldn't struggle. All the verses the Sterns taught her, all the advice from crisis training vanished. Her mind screamed out Simon's name, but he wasn't here. There was no way he could help her now. God alone would witness her fate. She lifted her chin up to the heavens, where clouds blocked all but the faintest traces of starlight.

He led her away from the van. She stumbled on her broken leg and collapsed to the ground. Soon knelt down beside her and touched her swollen ankle. She scooted away but knew her situation was hopeless. She didn't even beg for mercy. She ignored the tears of fear and shame that stung her eyes. Maybe she was lucky to be sick. She was so weak and miserable, she wouldn't mind dying here.

Soon stood up. He lifted his empty palms in a posture of surrender. "I'm so sorry, Sister. I have no intention of hurting you. I promise."

She shut her eyes, hoping her fever would sweep her away into delirium.

He remained a few paces away. "I won't hurt you."

Her body trembled too hard for her to trust his words. When he took a step forward, she crawled back with a tiny sob.

"Please, try to listen." He hung his head and squatted down. "I'm only trying to help you. This is all part of the plan."

She wondered if this was some sort of strange miracle. Maybe God had allowed her mind to escape into an entirely new reality while her body suffered the unthinkable. Would she wake up when it was over? Would she remember the shame that had been committed against her?

"I had to take my shirt off." Soon wrapped his arms around his chest. "It was bugged." Hannah frowned. If she was hallucinating, why did he use words she didn't know? "They put devices in our uniforms when we're off premises to record what we're doing." He gestured back to his pile of clothes. "I didn't have any other way to speak with you freely." Her body still trembled. "I'm a believer. Just like you. I was saved not too long ago by the influence of ... of someone in Chongjin." He swallowed hard. "I was supposed to take you to the gulag. That's not going to happen. But if my superiors get curious and wonder where you went, you see, they can just listen to the recordings and make certain assumptions and ... and ..." He wiped his forehead.

"That was for a recording?"

"I'm so sorry. Please forgive me. If I could think of any other way, I would have. I would never hurt you. I promise."

"But you work for the jail?"

He shook his head. "I can't explain everything. It wouldn't be safe. For either of us." She frowned but let out her breath while he continued. "This is the Tumen River. You're directly across a village called Sanhe. There's a man there, Mr. Kim. He runs a safe house for refugees. He'll be expecting you."

"How will I find him?" The breeze slapped her hair across her face.

"We're standing almost exactly opposite where he lives. Cross the river, then go straight up the path. You'll come to a large grove of thorn bushes. Beyond that is a house with a cross in the window. Look carefully; it's behind a sheer curtain. Go to Mr. Kim and tell him you came from Chongjin."

She studied the river. Its current wasn't strong, but there was no way to ford it on her injured leg. "How will I get across?"

"We have a boat. You'll have to row yourself to the other side, then hide it as well as you can. We'll have someone else come and take care of it later." He looked at her leg. "You have to hurry. The sun will be up soon. The border patrolmen will be making their rounds."

She shook her head, trying to focus. "What about Simon?"

He lowered his gaze. "It just wasn't possible to save you both."

She heard the words through a feverish haze. "He'll be coming later, then?"

"I'm afraid not."

Hannah was no longer chilled. Beads of perspiration dotted her forehead. "Why?"

Soon still crouched, hugging himself to cover his naked chest. "There's a reason you were chosen."

She was thirsty. She longed to plunge her face into the river and drink.

"You were strong," Soon insisted. "During all the interrogations, you didn't waver."

She felt his words would be easy to grasp if she weren't so exhausted. She tried to study his face, but it was spinning around in her field of vision.

"The underground church needs workers with your courage and stamina." She wiped her brow, hoping to clear her head so she could understand better.

Soon took a deep breath. "For now, only one thing matters.

Get yourself to the safe house. Find Mr. Kim. Once you're healthy again, someone will contact you."

Hannah didn't ask what he meant. She only knew she needed sleep. Hot tea, sleep, and in the morning maybe something to eat. She brushed the dirt off her clothes. "Where's that boat?"

She would never have guessed how painful it would be to row with a broken leg. She struggled against the oars, biting the inside of her cheek to keep from crying out. It took all her energy just to keep from veering downstream. She was glad the current was slow. In some areas, the river was so shallow she could jam her oar into the bottom of the silty riverbed and push herself off. By the time she reached the other side, the throbbing in her bone radiated all the way up to her hip and made her empty stomach churn. The physical activity helped clear away the fever's heaviness, but that only made her more acutely aware of the pain in her leg.

"Hold me in your hands, I depend on you."

She collapsed onto the embankment with a subdued sob. Her swollen throat threatened to close up entirely. With each inhalation, she prayed for comfort and courage.

"Hold me in your hands. Carry me through."

Her ankle was swollen to twice its regular size. It was just as well she gave her boots away back in Yanji, because she could never wear them again until her leg healed. She glanced over the riverbank. Soon was already gone. She stared up the path and wondered how long it would take if she had to crawl the whole way to Mr. Kim's.

"When the road is rough and I stumble and I fall ..."

It was just past dawn when she finally reached the grove of trees Soon mentioned. She dropped down near a copse of thorn bushes and counted out five deep breaths. She would make it. She had to. Maybe somehow her work on this side of the border would atone for her failure back home. Maybe she would find a way to make Simon and the Sterns proud.

"When my eyes are blinded by the tears that fall ..."

She needed God to protect her. She needed his shelter, his encouragement. Every part of her longed to collapse right there underneath the thorn bushes. Perhaps God would send an angel to tend to her leg while she slept. Or maybe he would take pity on her and bring her home to heaven right now. She wouldn't regret dying here. Simon would probably join her soon enough.

"You pick me up and carry me through."

In time, her breathing slowed down. She was chilled all the way to her bone marrow, but she didn't tremble so violently. She spotted a house in the distance. A flickering candle in the window cast shadows from a small cross. She took a deep breath and hobbled toward shelter.

CHAPTER 11

"What do you want?"

Noting the stranger's severe frown, Hannah wondered if she arrived at the wrong home. From behind him, a young girl peeked up from her sweeping and then quickly lowered her eyes back to the floor. Hannah placed her hand on the doorframe to steady herself. Everything in her field of vision spun in radiating spirals. "Are you Mr. Kim?"

He inclined his head at the slightest angle, a gesture Hannah expected was his impression of a bow. Since he made no move to say anything else, she bowed and continued, "I was sent here. From Chongjin." She strained to see if the cross she spied in the copse still hung in the window. The metallic clink of prison doors echoed dully in her mind, and she made herself relax her clammy hands.

He crossed his arms as he inspected her. She instinctively held her breath as his disapproving glare traveled from her hair to the ragged prison clothes still stained with blood. He grunted and stepped back from the open doorway. "No use standing on the porch."

Her throat constricted as she entered the home. There were no cement walls, no meter-high cages where victims were made to crouch like animals, no solitary confinement cells where darkness and silence threatened to steal away a prisoner's last remnants of humanity. A chicken clucked from somewhere out back, and a kettle of water boiled on top of the stove. Hannah tried to swallow. She had only taken two steps into the room before Mr. Kim reached behind her and swung the door shut.

He shrugged toward a chair by a small table. "Sit."

The young girl continued with her sweeping, but Hannah caught her staring and gave a small smile. She thought of her flower-swallows, the street children she had cared for during the worst of the Great Hardship. She remembered the ones who died in her arms after their weak, rattling lungs finally surrendered, the ones she couldn't wake up after a cold night spent huddled like newborn kittens in abandoned sheds. She thought of little Woong, his sing-songy voice, his mischievous face that always managed to get smudged with dirt and grime. She remembered how skinny his arms grew those last days before he disappeared. How old would Woong be now? She tried to calculate it out. Had the Sterns' warm blankets and fatty meals dulled her memory?

"Tea?" Mr. Kim's voice sounded far too gruff to offer such a luxury, but she glanced up at the balding man and nodded.

She thought of the churches she visited the first time she crossed the border into China. How many had sent her away before someone finally pointed her to the Sterns'?

"Yes, thank you."

He cleared his throat. Hannah smiled once more at the girl, but the child swept on and stared at her with sad, shallow eyes. Hannah recognized the expression all too well.

After pouring some drinks, Mr. Kim sat across from her at the small kitchen table. "You will wake up with the sunrise."

The teacup in her hand trembled just a little. Did that mean he was going to let her stay?

"When your leg is healed, you will tend to the chickens. Until then, you can weave baskets with my daughter. Your tasks will also include meal preparation."

Hannah opened her mouth to voice her willingness to help, but he didn't slow down enough to let her speak.

"You are to eat only at appointed meal times. And if other ..."

Here Mr. Kim paused, as if searching for a lost word. He coughed once before continuing. "If other persons come to the safe house, for whatever reason, you are to remain in your room with the door closed. You will not listen to outside conversations. You will not ask questions, not of me, not of my daughter, and not of our guests." He lowered his gaze. "It's for your own safety."

She blinked into her teacup. The bottom half of her leg was swollen like a bloated corpse, and the pain stabbed at her shin and burned its way up to the side of her hip. She felt her body swaying slightly but couldn't steady herself. "I understand, sir." She wondered what would happen if she forgot one of Mr. Kim's countless edicts.

He scowled at her interruption. "My daughter, So-Young, is barely more than a child." Hannah glanced toward where the girl had been cleaning, but she was gone. Mr. Kim waited until Hannah turned back around before he went on. "My daughter knows very little about life outside of Sanhe. I expect it to remain that way. Indefinitely." He leveled his eyes, and Hannah felt like she was already being punished for some unknown transgression.

"I understand," she assured him in a voice hardly louder than a whisper. She sipped her tea and winced as it scalded the back of her throat. She had gotten used to honey with her tea, the way Mrs. Stern always prepared it. She hadn't had tea of any kind in weeks, not since her meeting with Mr. Tong. She pictured the old man's leathery skin, remembered his prayer for her before she left him, recalled his butchered corpse. Her heart was sore, heavy, as if someone was wringing it out like a sopping-wet rag.

Mr. Kim stood and scraped his chair out behind him. Hannah wasn't sure if she was supposed to follow him or not. He frowned at her swollen leg. "My daughter will tend to your injuries." At his words, So-Young's shy face peered out from around a corner. He grunted at her, and she scurried toward the table.

Moving deftly, So-Young glided a chair in front of Hannah and then retreated to the bedroom. Mr. Kim crossed his arms.

She returned seconds later with two pillows, which she propped on the chair. "I'm sorry if this hurts you."

It was the first time Hannah heard her voice, which sounded more mature than her small frame and timid ways suggested. She lifted Hannah's leg onto the cushions.

"Is it very painful?"

Hannah squeezed her eyes shut. The sound of clinking chains, the smell of mold on the cold concrete walls, the metallic taste of blood were less than a day old in her memory, and this wispy child felt bad for propping her leg up on some pillows. "I'm fine." She summoned a smile to ease So-Young's mind. "Thank you."

So-Young beamed. "I just need a few more things."

Mr. Kim scowled at his daughter and strode out of the room.

A few minutes after So-Young finished wrapping some cold rags and a homemade splint around Hannah's leg, a young man entered the house. Hannah could barely see him from where she sat at the kitchen table, but she felt his presence fill the room as soon as she heard the door swing open. He was tall and lanky, Hannah noted as soon as he stepped into her field of vision. He was built so much like Simon, a quick surge of elation jolted through her body, replaced almost immediately with the heavy sting of disappointment. She shut her eyes once. Simon was gone, broken, lost somewhere in the North Korean network of gulags — if he was still alive at all. How would she ever know? Would her heart tell her if he were dead, or would she live with this dreadful uncertainty forever?

The young man looked in all directions at once, a smile on his gaunt face. "I've come, Uncle!" High cheekbones held up a pair of wiry glasses. He carried a box, heavy if you judged by the way he grimaced when he set it down in the entryway. His eyes darted across the kitchen, barely registered Hannah, and landed on So-

Young. "Little Cousin!" He swirled his fingers around in the air before he pulled out a small piece of taffy from his pants pocket. So-Young let out a tiny giggle and hurried toward him. He tousled her hair and held the candy just out of reach. She stretched her arms up and jumped with a squeal before her father's disapproving grunt ended the jocularity.

"Nephew Kwan." Mr. Kim dipped his head down, and the young man returned with a more formal bow.

"It's good to see you, Uncle." Kwan spanned the space between them in two short strides and clasped the portly man on both shoulders. So-Young tugged on Kwan's arm, and he handed over the candy. "It's peppermint. Your favorite." Her face crinkled up in a soundless giggle, and Hannah's heart ached for the days she had laughed with the other students at the Sterns' Secret Seminary. They would never be together again. "I see you have a guest," Kwan noted, finally turning to Hannah.

Mr. Kim crossed his arms. "Daughter, show our new arrival to the spare room. Take the pillows with you."

So-Young scurried to Hannah's side. "Can you walk a little ways?" Her voice was full of compassion, with no hint of her previous giddiness.

Earlier that morning, Hannah had rowed herself across the Tumen River and stumbled uphill to the safe house, dragging her leg behind her. "Yes, I can walk." She let So-Young prop her up by the elbow. The young man Kwan rushed to take her other arm. His physical closeness, the kind expression on his face, even his refusal to ask any questions, made Hannah feel wretched. She remembered clenching Simon's hand when they found each other in the Chongjin cell. She knew at that moment he would have done anything for her. He had done everything for her, even betrayed innocent believers. Was that to be her last memory of him, a burden to carry forever and never shed until death? She sniffed once, and Kwan paused.

"Are you all right?"

Hannah thought of Simon's anguished cry when they were torn apart from one another, its resonance echoing bitterly against the cement walls of the prison chamber.

She nodded once and shuffled to the bedroom. She hardly noticed Kwan lifting her onto the bed; she didn't register the softness of the mattress beneath her. Her thoughts were consumed with Simon, the words they never spoke, the work they never accomplished. Had she failed him? Had she been a stumbling block to him like Jesus had warned his disciples about? She rolled onto her side and couldn't even thank So-Young for the warm blanket tucked in around her shivering body. So-Young and Kwan slipped out without a word, and Hannah shed large, hot tears that did nothing to soothe her aching spirit.

CHAPTER 12

As sunlight poured in through the small window, Hannah slept. She dreamed she was swinging in the hammock in Mrs. Stern's garden. The sun enveloped her in its rays and warmed her all the way to the center of her being. The pain in her leg was gone; her stomach was full. The sweet, earthy scent of marigolds blended with the heady fragrance of jasmine. The roses were in bloom. From inside, she heard the murmured prayers of the other Secret Seminary students.

He came up behind her like a soft breeze and stroked her cheek with his finger. A sudden, delightful chill pricked at her neck, and the leaves rustled above them. She reached up and touched his hand, closed her eyes, and breathed in his smell. "Shouldn't you be in there with the rest of them?" His voice was distant, muffled somehow. She couldn't tell if his tone was accusatory or not.

She strained her ears. Inside the house, their comrades interceded with fervor for the leaders of North Korea, for refugees trying to escape, for believers in prison camps. "We better go inside," she whispered. She made a move to get up, but her body was too heavy, the air itself weighing her down like layer after layer of quilts.

"Do we have to?" She heard the smile in his voice as he joined her in the hammock. Waves of heat danced up her back as he snuggled up behind her, curled up against her, wrapped his arms around her. The hammock swayed, but there was plenty of room for them to share. She had never been so close to him before, but it was familiar, like a cup of Mrs. Stern's sweetened tea — just the right temperature, perfectly steeped.

His fingers glided slowly through her hair. Her head rested on the soft spot between his shoulder and bicep. "I want to stay here," she confessed. "I don't want to go anywhere."

"Me, either." His lips brushed against her ear, the sensation of that first tender kiss shooting tendrils of ice and comfort that eventually settled down deep in her belly.

When Hannah woke up, her pillow was soaked in tears, and she shivered from the cold.

***

Simon's body slumped to the floor. His limbs ached, but he knew his injuries paled in comparison to what Hannah endured during the past two weeks in Chongjin. He gritted his teeth, wishing he could smash his head against the concrete wall and end his miserable, pitiful existence. The mere thought of her threatened to steal away his last remnants of sanity. He remembered her eyes, always so trusting, so gentle. In the past, her tender gaze had been enough to encourage him, comfort him, embolden him. He wasn't even sure he would have completed his training if she hadn't stared at him so often with such frank admiration. Giving up hadn't been an option. When she looked at him, she saw a saint. A hero.

Now she knew what he really was.

Shame pressed down on him like the lid on a coffin. How could he ever stand tall again? How could he continue on after failing the woman he loved? Yes, he loved her. He had always loved her. From that first night in Mrs. Stern's garden, that first conversation they shared, his heart belonged to her. He tried to fight it, deceived himself into believing his emotions were under control. He had ignored his heart and tried to reason his affection away. He could never be with her. He had swallowed down his love, and now he found himself drowning in a tsunami of regrets and impossible yearnings.

He loved her. How easily he could admit it to himself now, when both their lives were forfeit. He loved her, and that's why he couldn't lift his head anymore. If he had been able to keep tighter control over his emotions, if he had followed through with his mission instead of charging after her like a gallant, errant fool, she would have never been caught. It was his fault she was captured, his love for her that put her through such unthinkable torment. And yet, if he had to make those choices again, he would only be fated to watch himself repeat the same offenses a hundred times over.

He loved her, and now that he acknowledged the truth, he knew he would never find a way to stop loving her. It was just as well God took her away. Such idols need to be exorcised entirely, plucked like weeds before they have a chance to grow and choke out all surrounding life. A love like theirs could never find fulfillment. A love like theirs could only end in tragedy.

He couldn't tell if it was day or night when the two men forced their way into his dark cell and yanked off his ankle cuffs. He hadn't eaten in days, refusing the cold gruel the guard passed under the slats of his cage. He didn't care about food, didn't care about relieving himself in his little tin pail, didn't care that his skin was blistering with infection. When the two men lifted him to his feet, he felt no fear. They would kill him eventually. Why not today? Simon was nothing more than a stopwatch. With only a few ticks left on the second-hand, did it matter what happened before his time finally ran out?

He hated his legs for supporting his weight as he followed the guards down the hall. He had to stop thinking about Hannah and her twisted leg, the way she hobbled away from him. He had to stop thinking about the curve of her shoulders and the gentleness in her eyes. He had to stop thinking about the way she hugged him in the woods, the feel of her skin as they clasped hands in the dark. He shook his head, wishing to rattle the memories loose and be rid of them forever. His love for her was a weakness that had to be carved out of his heart permanently.

He was weeping by the time the men led him outside the Chongjin jail, but he didn't notice the blinding light of the afternoon sun or the bitter wind stinging his cheeks. He didn't notice the rough hands that shoved him into the van or the smell of old gasoline and exhaust. All he thought about was Hannah, the one he had vowed to exorcise from his heart, the one he could never stop thinking about no matter how hard he tried.

When the van started moving, Simon barely saw anything. He lost track of how long they had been driving and only remembered the sadness in Hannah's eyes when he last saw her. A thousand reprimands shot from her gaze and pierced his soul like a torturer's needle. He would welcome the interrogation chair if it could rip away that single memory.

Eventually, they arrived at a mass of barbed wire as tall as a man. A guard stationed at the gate waved them through, and Simon counted six more patrolmen stationed in watchtowers. The van passed through each of the security checkpoints without event. Simon straightened in his seat. Two men in drab gray prison uniforms slumped along, each laden with a large bucket that sloshed its contents onto their bare feet. Some young children gathered in a little huddle, picking up sticks. A pig in a sty behind them poked its nose around in the dirt. The animal was the only creature in sight that didn't look like it was starving.

The van eventually stopped in front of a squat building. A sign flapped in the breeze: *Administration.* Simon thought about what comfort he could whisper to Hannah, and he had to remind himself yet again she was gone. It was like the loss of a limb. He might never fully get over his phantom urges to talk with her. He thought of their last night together in Yanji, lifetimes removed from interrogations and starvation and failed missions. *"There are no good-byes in the kingdom of heaven,"* she had breathed so confidently. If only they had known back then what awaited them.

The men prodded him out of the van with slow, lazy movements. They held him by both elbows, but he walked himself up to the administration building. He had failed the believers he was sent to serve. He had failed Hannah. Now he would pay for his mistakes, but at least he could still carry himself. He wouldn't let them drag him to his fate like a coward. One of the guards swung the front door open, and he made sure to cross the threshold before anyone else.

A tired-looking man whose cap was several sizes too large glanced up from a thick file. Without ceremony, the guard passed him a sealed envelope. The clerk opened it with a yawn, and once he finished perusing it, he fixed his gaze on Simon.

"You are at Camp 22. You are prisoner number 39846." The corner of his eye twitched. "You're here until you die."

CHAPTER 13

It was close to evening by the time Hannah's full bladder finally forced her to limp out of the bedroom. Mr. Kim sat hunched over the box the young man brought over earlier. He straightened and cleared his throat.

Hannah blushed. "I ... I guess your company has left." Mr. Kim's brow furrowed even deeper, but he said nothing. She had never been particularly close to Mr. Stern, but she missed the American's fatherly ways. She swallowed, grateful her throat wasn't quite as raw. She looked around once, hoping to catch a glimpse of So-Young. "Your daughter is ...?"

"Making a delivery."

Hannah wasn't sure if she should keep on standing there or just hobble back to her room. She couldn't stop shivering. Her head throbbed. A wave of relief soothed her burning cheeks when the front door opened, and So-Young dashed in, just barely dodging one of the chairs near the entryway. Kwan rushed after her, his arms high above his head, his growls and snarls intermingled with snorts of laughter.

"Daughter!" Mr. Kim barked, but it took So-Young another several seconds to gain control of her momentum. She was panting and laughing at the same time, and her squeals only intensified when Kwan picked her up over his head with a deafening roar. Hannah felt Mr. Kim's displeasure, waves of irritation the two playfellows either couldn't detect or chose to ignore. When So-Young's giggles finally subsided, Kwan set her upright on her feet.

"That's enough," Mr. Kim mumbled. Nobody responded.

"Will you be staying the night, Brother Kwan?" So-Young tugged on his hand.

During the Great Hardship, Hannah used to joke that her family of adopted flower-swallows would one day pull her shoulder out of joint from yanking her so hard like that. She took a deep breath, hoping to ease the heaviness of her memories. Yes, there had been laughter then, too. The children weren't so physically boisterous, but when they were lucky enough to find scraps to fill their distended bellies, they could make a commotion to rival the safe-house cacophony.

Kwan lifted his arm as So-Young held on, letting her legs dangle several centimeters off the floor. Hannah was surprised by his strength. All the other Koreans she knew were from the North, where even the village police were malnourished weaklings. "I've got to cross one more time," Kwan answered. "Moses ..."

Everyone stopped. Their heads snapped toward Hannah. So-Young straightened her legs and stood on her own feet. Her smile faded, and she took a small step behind Kwan. He brought his hands together and cracked several of his knuckles one after the other. "That is ... I meant ..."

The heat from Mr. Kim's scowl was directed at the young man, but it radiated outward and made Hannah's neck burn. She was about to excuse herself when Mr. Kim looked at So-Young. "Daughter, show our arrival where the outhouse is."

A few minutes later, Hannah hobbled back to her room, where the view of the two men was blocked but not the sound.

"I still don't know what Moses was thinking." Mr. Kim's volume had steadily increased.

She did what she could to keep from eavesdropping, but the fine hairs on the back of her neck stood on end, and she couldn't ignore their words.

"She can't even be twenty years old. Next thing you know,

he'll expect me to send my own daughter across the border."

"Moses has a reason for everything he does." Kwan's voice was steady, and Hannah longed to let her soul absorb its confidence.

Mr. Kim laughed mirthlessly. "He has reasons, sure enough."

"His situation is ... precarious." Hannah noted the reverence in Kwan's voice. "He's constantly in danger."

Mr. Kim grunted. "So am I. But you don't see me plucking little girls out of nursery school and throwing them to the Pyongyang tigers."

Hannah wished she could ignore their conversation, but even though her head was heavy with fever and her body trembled with chills underneath the blanket, her mind tuned in to every syllable.

"She came from Chongjin," Kwan stated. "She obviously endured a lot at the jail. She must have proven herself to someone over there, gotten Moses' attention somehow. They say he has connections within ..."

"I don't need to be told about his connections," Mr. Kim spat. The conversation ended for a moment, and when it resumed, the whispers were too faint for Hannah to decipher.

Throughout the rest of the evening, So-Young tiptoed in every now and then to pat down Hannah's clammy forehead with a cool rag or offer some bitter tea. As she nursed Hannah's fever and injured leg, So-Young might have passed as a teenager if she weren't so tiny. Other times, like when she giggled and played with Kwan, she didn't seem a day older than Woong and the other flower-swallows Hannah had cared for so many years ago. Were any of them still alive? She had lost count of how many she had buried before she finally crossed the border and found her way to the Sterns'.

"She won't be able to make any deliveries until that leg heals." Hannah overheard Mr. Kim's remark and wondered if he already regretted her presence here, if he begrudged her the two cups of tea and splint she had claimed her first day as his guest.

"I doubt she's ready to go out yet, anyway," Kwan replied. "She needs time to heal."

Hannah shut her eyes, wondering what they'd say if they knew she was listening.

"She's been through a lot ..."

"The girl's safe now," Mr. Kim interrupted. "She should be grateful to have a roof over her head, not an unmarked tombstone."

Hannah wished So-Young would return with more tea. Her throat was parched.

Kwan stayed for supper that evening, and So-Young prepared a vegetable dish and hearty broth soup. The conversation was sparse. Kwan's trivial chatter invited nothing but angry murmurs from Mr. Kim at the head of the table. Hannah thought back to the dinner conversations in Yanji, the theological debates Mr. Stern was so happy to moderate, the times when she and Simon broke away from the others to share a private moment in the midst of such boisterous fellowship. Hannah couldn't offer Kwan more than a passing glance. He reminded her too much of Simon. It wasn't his build exactly. She had studied him further and decided he was more wiry and angular than Simon, but both young men possessed a strengthening, calming presence. The similarity between them embarrassed her for some reason she couldn't articulate.

She sipped at her soup but had lost her appetite. Her fever was improving by the hour, the result perhaps of So-Young's herbal concoction, but the meal was far too spicy. When was the last time Simon ate anything but prison gruel? Did the guards bother to feed him at all anymore? She thought of their last moment together, when his tormented cry followed her out of the interrogation room. He called out her name, but what was left for them to say in such a short time? She played through those last seconds, the things she might have told him. She wanted him to know how sorry she was. She would never stop blaming herself for distracting him from his mission. It would have been better if the two of them had never met again after crossing the border.

Something beeped, a strange electronic noise. Mr. Kim fumbled in his pocket and pulled out a small phone. He squinted and frowned. "I have to go." He scraped his chair out behind him. "I'll be back later."

A pang of guilt pricked Hannah's conscience when she realized she was relieved to see him depart. The mood around the table relaxed almost immediately after he left.

"How is your wound?" It was the first time Kwan spoke directly to her all night.

"I think it's going to heal up just fine." Inwardly, she blamed the flush creeping up her face on her subsiding fever.

"And your ..." Kwan stared into his lap and cracked a knuckle. "How is everything else?"

She wasn't sure what he already knew about her, but the question left her skin cold and clammy. "So-Young is taking very good care of me." She wasn't certain if this was the sort of response he expected or not.

He leaned back in his chair. "You must have made quite an impression at Chongjin. They hardly ever send women to us and never anyone so young."

Hannah felt she should reply somehow, but the words got jumbled in her mouth. "I had a friend there," she muttered. "In the jail."

Kwan nodded. "I'm sorry you were separated from each other." His penetrating glance suggested he knew more about the situation than Hannah would have wished.

"So Mr. Kim is your uncle?" She had to keep her mind off Simon.

"He's my mentor. We're not actually related." Kwan took a

noisy slurp of soup before declaring, "Little Sister, your cooking grows more and more delicious every time I visit."

Hannah forgot her own discomfort when she saw the deep red inching its way all the way up to the tips of So-Young's ears. Kwan grinned and reached under his chair. "I brought you a birthday present, by the way."

So-Young's flush morphed into a childish beam that lit up her entire face. She clasped her hands in front of her. "You remembered!"

Kwan laughed easily. "How could I forget my favorite eleven year-old?" He pulled out a small bundle wrapped in thin paper. "Happy birthday."

So-Young grabbed the package with both hands and let out a delightful squeal. Shreds of paper fell to the ground until she held a small doll in the crook of her arms. "She's perfect."

So-Young glowed adoringly at her gift, Kwan beamed proudly, and Hannah realized she was a stranger, witnessing a moment entirely unfit for outsiders.

CHAPTER 14

"You're called Simon, right?"

Simon ignored the old man and kept working. He had already learned after just three days in the mines nothing positive ever came from conversing with another prisoner. He wasn't Simon anymore. He was 39846. His only purpose in life was to keep from falling behind. There was nothing more important than keeping up. If the overseer didn't beat you for failing to meet quota, your fellow slaves took matters into their own hands. Simon's physical build seemed suited for mining, but he still hadn't fallen into rhythm with the others. He ignored his comrade's question and continued to dig as the shouts of the overseer reverberated just around a dark corner.

"My name's Mal-Chin." The man's voice sounded stronger than his white hair and leathery skin suggested. Simon glanced at the stranger's nearly-full wheelbarrow and wondered how anybody could work that fast. "You just arrived."

It wasn't a question. Simon was already infamous in his unit, since his work resulted in reduced rations for them all. He had already endured all the vengeance he could swallow from his hungry comrades and ignored the introduction. A bead of sweat dropped off his forehead. He had learned within his first hour working here that stopping to wipe your brow was an unpardonable offense.

"Do you bear the cross?" Mal-Chin's whisper was so soft Simon wondered if he just imagined the words. The old man was focused on his labor, and for several minutes the only sound to be heard was the chink of the shovels and the thudding of the overseer's boots behind them.

"Do you bear the cross?" Mal-Chin repeated the question after the overseer turned down the next winding passage, taking most of the light with him. The words were soft but articulate. Simon didn't respond. Was Mal-Chin some sort of National Security Agency plant, an informer paid to tip his superiors off about subversives? That might explain how strong he was in spite of his age. Or was he speaking in some kind of secret code, known only to Christian prisoners? Simon kept his mouth shut, the stranger's questions ceased, and he met quota for the first time since he arrived at Camp 22.

***

When he crossed the border back into North Korea, Simon knew he might one day die for preaching the gospel. He never expected to be murdered for working too slow.

The overseer angled his boot so the kick landed on the underside of Simon's ribs. Simon raised his hand before the blunt side of a shovel smashed down into his cheek. His vision deserted him, and blood spurted out of his nose. He tried to turn his head, but his fellow prisoners now joined the attack, either emboldened by the overseer's example or too frightened to show any mercy.

Hannah's name was on the tip of his lips, but he refused to utter it before such vicious brutes, men stripped of all dignity until only animalistic instincts remained. He was the weakling. His lags over the past two weeks meant reduced rations for everyone. There was no forgiveness here in Camp 22, only death, death without Hannah, death without purpose, death at the hands of creatures who could hardly be held accountable for their actions. *Forgive them, Father, for they do not know what they do.* He curled up into himself, protecting his organs as best as he could. He gagged on pools of blood. *Air.* He needed more air.

"Enough." The voice carried over the deafening ringing in Simon's ear. The assault abated long enough for him to throw up. His vision came back in blotchy patches, and he saw the white-haired prisoner bend over him. Mal-Chin placed one hand under his neck, another under his knees, and then scooped him up as easily as if Simon had been a baby.

"Enough."

Fog darkened Simon's mind, a heaviness seeped through his body, and his consciousness slipped away like a dream that fades into mist at sunrise.

When he woke up, it took Simon several minutes to remember what happened. "Take a sip, Brother," a voice prompted. The cool liquid dribbled down Simon's chin. The light burned his retinas. He blinked.

Simon directed all his energy to his sense of vision, forcing his eyes to focus on the face leaning over him. "Hannah?"

A soft laugh. "No, my friend, although I imagine she's a prettier sight than I." Simon blinked again. The man let out his breath. "You've been calling out for her, you know. I'm sorry she's not here."

It hurt Simon to speak his name. "Mal-Chin." He squeezed his eyes to shut out the agonizing white light. He remembered the shouts and the shovels of his angry comrades and groaned once.

"Drink a little more." Mal-Chin brought another spoonful to his lips, but Simon couldn't taste anything but blood. Mal-Chin wiped drool off Simon's chin. "Do you remember where you are?"

Simon winced before croaking his answer. "Camp."

"I wish I could tell you otherwise."

"How ... How long?" The side of Simon's head hurt so much he feared if he touched it, he'd find it as squishy as an over-ripe melon.

"Day and a half," Mal-Chin answered. "We made quota

yesterday, so we're back to full rations." There was a smile in his voice that reminded Simon of something.

"You helped me."

Mal-Chin patted his shoulder. "You should sleep now. Tomorrow you're back in the mines."

***

He worked in spite of his broken body because he knew he wouldn't survive another beating. One eye was still swollen halfway shut. Pain seared through his bruised ribs with each heave of the shovel. Mal-Chin worked beside him, dropping one scoop of coal in Simon's barrel for every two he hoisted into his own.

"Thank you," Simon whispered.

"For what?" Mal-Chin shrugged, and Simon didn't say anything else for the rest of his shift.

That evening, Mal-Chin laid a strong hand on Simon's shoulder as the men returned to their dorm. "You did well today."

Simon glanced behind to see how far they were from the overseer and other prying ears. "You didn't have to help me."

Mal-Chin shrugged once more. "Did if I didn't want them to cut back on rations again."

"It was good of you." Simon swallowed once, unsure if uttering the next word was reckless or brave. "Brother."

Mal-Chin drew closer. He flicked some dirt off the sleeve of his uniform. After a small group of men sauntered past, he cleared his throat. "We're meeting tonight. Should I wake you?"

Simon's hands went clammy, and he raised a finger to the soft spot on the side of his head. "Tonight?"

Mal-Chin nodded.

Simon remembered the way Hannah's throat quivered when the junior guillotine's blade pressed against her finger. "Where?"

Mal-Chin rubbed his chin and frowned. "Will you join us?"

Simon shut his eyes for a moment. His body ached, and his only real desire was for sleep. He let his breath out slowly. "Yeah, go ahead and wake me up." His head throbbed, and he hoped he wouldn't regret his decision.

A few hours later, Simon's subconscious had just reached that dark place without dreams, without pain, that merciful no man's land where neither hope nor fear exist, when a strong hand shook him awake. There were no lights in the dorm, but he recognized Mal-Chin's voice. "It's time."

There was no way to tell the hour. Simon's body was heavy. When he tried to rise, exhaustion created its own kind of gravity that tugged him back toward the floor. Mal-Chin clasped his hand and pulled him up, reminding Simon he was still alive, he still had work to carry on. He stood with his bare feet on the concrete floor and shuffled past the piles of sleeping bodies, the prisoners whose only purpose was to serve the Party. Simon was new enough to Camp 22 he still dreamed of escape, he still hoped for that impossible freedom which beckoned to him even in the belly of the earth where he mined for the National Security Agency. Less than a month ago, he had eaten pork and steak at the Sterns', with rice smothered in sweet sauce and crispy vegetables fresh from the market. During the Great Hardship, before he joined the Secret Seminary, his stomach had distended and cramped up just as much as anyone else's. But experiencing hunger was harder now after spending an entire year well-fed and nourished. He thought about the meal packs Hannah gave away to the street children in Yanji, and he wondered what food she had to eat wherever she was now.

"Stop for a minute." Mal-Chin let go of Simon's hand and crouched down in a back corner. No one slept this far away from the central heater, but the men's voices would still carry if they tried to talk. No one would dare meet out here in the open. Simon heard a click coming from ground level. A faint light jutted from a crack in the floor. "Down here." Mal-Chin gestured with his hand. Simon squatted and saw the ladder leading down to a sort of cellar, and he made his descent as quickly as possible. Mal-Chin followed and shut the trap door after them.

Below ground, Simon held onto the ladder for support and looked around. About a dozen prisoners crouched near a small lantern, the kind used down in the mines. Simon examined the men more closely and noted one with the small red stripe on his uniform that set him apart as an overseer. Most of the prisoners returned his scrutiny with a mix of mistrustful frowns or curious gazes. Someone from his own unit kept his eyes on his boots. Simon reached to the area by his temple where the shovel had smashed him. Mal-Chin gestured to an empty spot on the floor, and he sat, quivering slightly from the cold.

"You're Simon," the overseer stated flatly.

"We always pray and vote before inviting in new members," Mal-Chin explained and sat down beside him.

"The votes aren't always unanimous." The overseer creased his brow.

Mal-Chin met his scowl with a serene gaze. "No, but we trust the Holy Spirit to guide our every decision." He confided in Simon in a lower tone, "We have to take every precaution, as you can ..."

The overseer cleared his throat. "Since we're all here, I suggest we start." He frowned at Simon. "What news do you have for us from outside?"

News? Simon had only been in North Korea for two weeks before his arrest. Most of that time he spent following Hannah and tracking the Christians she was supposed to meet, the same believers he himself betrayed. He wasn't about to share his failures with this panel of strangers, but they stared at him so intensely he felt he had to come up with something. Should he tell them about the Secret Seminary? He was already sentenced to a lifetime of hard labor in the Camp 22 mines. Would the officials increase his punishment if he confessed to associating with

Christian foreigners? His stomach churned. He had never considered himself a coward until he sneaked back home.

"What charges brought you here?" Mal-Chin's inquiry opened a floodgate of other questions from the curious men huddled around.

"Did you cross the border?"

"Have you ever met any missionaries?"

"Did you own a Bible before your arrest?"

"What can you tell us about Moses?"

This last question put an end to all others, and the men bent forward to hear Simon's answer. "Moses?" Simon turned questioningly to Mal-Chin, and several faces around the huddle fell.

"Moses," Mal-Chin repeated. "Miracle worker, champion of the underground church. Never heard of him?"

Simon shook his head. The overseer coughed. "Then it's time we got to praying, don't you think?" Murmurs of agreement rumbled around the circle. "That is, unless our new brother has any more information to impart." The overseer's tone seemed to carry both a question and an ultimatum.

Simon studied the prisoners around him. Had the Lord provided him with the fellowship his spirit needed to survive? Or was this another test of sorts? Were these men trustworthy? He couldn't even imagine what risks he had assumed simply by walking down that ladder. He wondered if Hannah would be proud of him if she knew where he was. The side of his head still throbbed.

CHAPTER 15

The ache in her leg woke Hannah hours before dawn. She had been dreaming of her wedding day. She wore the *hanbok* dress, and Mrs. Stern had arranged her hair with a tender and gentle touch. All their Secret Seminary friends were there, gathered in the Sterns' upstairs den. A light breeze wafted in the open windows, kissing her cheeks and making the frilly curtains dance. Mr. Stern held his large, black Bible, but Hannah couldn't hear his words. She couldn't focus on anything but Simon. He wore one of Mr. Stern's suits, and it swallowed up his hands like the gown he wore at the graduation ceremony right before they left Yanji. Hannah had just lifted her face to receive his kiss when the smarting in her bone stole the moment away from her forever.

She didn't stir, trying desperately to cling to his warmth and closeness. She held her breath, as if exhaling too hard might blow the memory of her dream away. Why did she torture herself with hollow hopes? His smell lingered in her mind even longer than the memory of his touch. She wished he were here, wished she could tell him how sorry she was. She needed him to know how much she missed him. Even now, when she prayed for him, she sensed only despair. She kept her eyes closed and tried to picture him. Where was he now? In the darkness, bent over the ground, a heaviness hanging over him like an invisible cage. She longed to go near to where he crouched. Maybe there was something she could say to him. Some way to encourage him.

"*When peace like a river attendeth my way ...*"

She pictured herself kneeling beside him, allowing her music to push back the discouragement, the fear, the exhaustion. She stretched out her hand, visualizing God's peace and healing flow through her fingers to wherever he was.

"When sorrows like sea billows roll..."

She imagined she was stroking his hair as she sang with a clarity and conviction she never experienced before. The heaviness lifted, gradually at first and then more dramatically. Her praise was a shield that encased them both. They were wrapped in its brilliance, dazzled by its majesty.

"Whatever my lot, thou hast taught me to say, 'It is well, it is well with my soul.'"

The moment was glorious, the first time she sensed the presence of the Holy Spirit so powerfully since she left the Secret Seminary. Exhausted, she wrapped the blankets around herself, thankful she had been able to share such a beautiful experience with Simon.

If only it had been him and not just a vision, it would have been a truly perfect moment.

***

At first, Simon didn't join in the prayers of the other prisoners as they huddled underneath the dorm. Other than Mal-Chin, they were all strangers. Who knew which ones might report back to the National Security Agency? Which one would turn them all in for an extra ration of gruel or a half-day vacation from the mines? He had already witnessed his own weaknesses. He didn't have any trust left in his fellow men, no matter how sincere their prayers sounded. Hadn't he once prayed just as fervently?

They extinguished the lamp, and Simon had to rely on his hearing alone to determine who was speaking. He immediately recognized Mal-Chin's voice, the gentle tenor that asked for grace and mercy on behalf of the camp guards. A few others prayed for loved ones — a sister who had already crossed the border into China, a son who had been imprisoned in a separate camp. Simon wondered who he should pray for. Orphaned during the Great Hardship, he hadn't had contact with any living relatives in years. He doubted he could find his uncles or grandparents even if he wanted to. He thought about the Sterns back in Yanji and silently asked God to bless their ministry, and he prayed for the other Secret Seminary students.

In the recesses of his mind, he remembered the last hymn they sang together in the Sterns' den, the evocative melody haunting him in this cold underground cellar. If he focused hard enough, he could almost hear Hannah's sweet soprano, and the skin on his shoulder tingled. He might never hear her sing again until they both were safe in heaven, but he clung to the memory like a shipwrecked sailor clutching at debris. The room fell silent, and Simon wondered if the others recognized how sacred that moment was. He held his breath and refused to move, afraid the moment would pass and he would realize Hannah wasn't actually next to him.

The following silence surrounded him like a vacuum, drawing the words from his throat.

"Though Satan should buffet, though trials should come ..."

He shut his eyes. If he sang some, maybe he could keep her memory from vanishing like vapor.

"Let this blessed assurance control ..."

His voice never rose above a hush, but he was joined by several others, men who had endured suffering and loss just as he had, but still found courage to rejoice in their Lord.

"That Christ has regarded my helpless estate and has shed his own blood for my soul."

When the song ended, no one spoke. Reluctantly, like men condemned to march back into a blizzard after basking in the warmth of a glorious fire, they opened the door to the cellar and returned in pairs and trios to where their comrades slept on, unaware that heaven had reached down to the bowels of the prison and freed men from their chains, if only for an instant.

From then on, Simon attended the underground meetings no matter how exhausted he was. He appreciated the fellowship and encouragement, but he went mostly to relive that first night when he could almost feel Hannah's breath on the back of his neck as she sang.

The men spent most of their time downstairs in prayer or Bible study. Simon and two of the others had memorized Scripture before their arrests, and the group worked together to learn as many passages as possible by heart. Simon had the most extensive reserve of them all, and the men were eager to tap into his mind's vast resources. One of his biggest fears was that he would forget some of the words before he could pass them on to others. He often wished for pen and paper, but it was far too dangerous to leave any tangible evidence of their treason.

In addition to Scripture memory work, the men sometimes talked of life outside the camp. One name came up more than any other.

"Who is this Moses everyone talks about?" Simon asked Mal-Chin one night after everyone else returned to the upper level.

"A deliverer." Simon couldn't see Mal-Chin, but he heard his friend adjust his position on the hard floor. "They say he's arranged for Christian leaders to escape the prison camps. Once, he even rescued an evangelist the night before he was sentenced to be hanged."

"Have you ever met him?"

"No," Mal-Chin answered. "No one here has."

Simon paused. "You're sure it's not just dreams of the condemned?"

He was thankful that the darkness hid the older man's face.

As the weeks passed in the mines, Simon found hope the most bitter tormenter of all. The sooner he could stop pining for Hannah, the easier it would be to submit to the guards' abuse, to switch off his mind, to shovel his coal like they demanded. He was homesick, not for a place, but for *her*, and nothing could cure him of his illness.

His question was answered by silence, and Simon worried for a moment he had offended his friend.

Finally, Mal-Chin took a deep breath. "If I didn't believe that someone on the outside was looking out for me, I'd go mad. Before working in the mines, I spent time in underground detainment. I witnessed things there ... heard things that would turn your hair just as white as mine." His voice grew even softer. "I survived on nothing but dreams, dreams that one day I would join my family again, dreams that somebody — Moses, an angel, God himself, I didn't care who — would see my suffering. Even if I was never set free, I just wanted someone on the outside to know where I was, to see me down here, to understand that I'm a real, flesh-and-blood man." Simon heard the tightness in his friend's throat. "I still dream, Brother. I have to. We all do. That's why if Moses doesn't exist, if he's just a legend we prisoners made up to hold onto foolish hope, I'd rather keep believing a lie than face such an awful truth."

Simon said nothing. He hoped Hannah would visit him tonight in his prayers and sing to him once more, but he knew only dreamless darkness awaited him like always.

CHAPTER 16

Soon's stomach flipped when General Sin swung open the door. "Why isn't the interrogation room ready?"

Soon jumped up, shuffling papers on top of his message from Mr. Kim in Sanhe. He hadn't had time to decipher the entire letter yet. He snapped to attention. "Yes, sir," he replied with what he hoped was enough enthusiasm. "I'll clean it right now."

He hurried out the door, grabbing the bucket and mop on his way. He wasn't sure which he hated more, getting the interrogation room ready or cleaning it up after a round of questioning. He knew it shouldn't matter to him, but it was always harder when the prisoners were Christian. Maybe it was because of the nightmares he had about taking his turn in the torture chair, his wrists and ankles bound with metal straps, his head locked in a restraint, his screams ripped out of his throat like those of so many other victims he had witnessed.

Before he slipped into the room, he spared a few extra seconds to raise his eyes to the chart on the door. *Transfer from Onsong. Name: Levi. Charged with espionage, threatening national security. Trained by American missionaries from Yanji.*

Soon swallowed hard. He had to get out of Chongjin.

***

General Sin lingered near Soon's desk. Soon was an idiot if he thought he could hide anything. General Sin's eyes were as sharp as a hawk's. Here in the Chongjin jail, he was omniscient.

He straightened the collar of his uniform. Nudging a few files over, he soon found the document Soon had tried to cover up. The encryption barely slowed down his reading.

H. arrived and is recovering her health. Should be ready for work by winter.

So the girl was at the Sanhe safe house now. Strange coincidence the news reached him right before he questioned another one of those American-trained "Secret Seminary" graduates. General Sin adjusted the papers on the desk. He'd deal with Soon later.

***

"I swear, I don't know what you're talking about."

Huge drops of sweat beaded on Levi's brow. Soon turned away, the bile rising up in his throat as he watched General Sin question the Christian prisoner. "We've already captured two of your comrades. We know all about your little 'Secret Seminary.' Your espionage training isn't quite a secret anymore, now, is it?"

The boy was shaking. Soon could hear his teeth chattering. "I don't know what you mean."

Soon had worked in Chongjin long enough to know this interrogation wouldn't last much longer. He already saw the blank look of defeat in the boy's eyes. Soon swallowed once, but it did nothing to soothe the disgust wedged in the back of his throat.

General Sin switched a small lever, and Soon had just enough time to brace himself before the prisoner's squeal reverberated off the walls. His writhing body reminded Soon of a squirrel shaken around in a dog's jaws. The general finally flicked the device off, and the only sound was of Levi's weak whimpering. General Sin stared down at him, his features etched in granite, his expression terrifying and cold. "You will give us the details of your mission. You will tell us everything you know. Who were you planning to meet?"

"Moses." The boy cleared his throat weakly. "I was trying to find Moses."

Soon's legs threatened to buckle beneath him. General Sin's expression was impossible to decode. He leaned in so close to the prisoner that Soon couldn't even see his lips move, but the general's growl rang out through the silence of the cell. "You lie."

Levi hung his head but said nothing.

"There is no Moses." General Sin grabbed the prisoner by the chin and forced his head up. "Who told you about Moses? Who fed you these lies? The Americans?" General Sin bellowed, his spittle landing on the prisoner's cheek.

Levi didn't respond. Was he still conscious? Soon leaned backward, his heart pounding. *Run.* Get away from Chongjin. Leave the jail forever. Flee the country. But his Party-relegated boots stuck fast to the hard, unyielding cement floor.

"Increase the voltage," General Sin demanded.

"I think he's passed out." Soon's voice frightened even himself. The general's head jerked up at its tiny squeak. "He's passed out," Soon insisted.

"Then call me when he wakes up." The general stormed out, slamming the door. Its echo shook the hollow space in Soon's chest.

***

General Sin's finger quivered once as he lit his cigarette. *Moses?* He slammed his fist onto his desk, jostling the pile of papers that loomed near the edge. *Moses!* He kicked the metal trash can and sent it clanging into one of his desk legs. Its contents spewed over.

Moses.

He glowered at the phone on his desk and took one more drag

before picking up the receiver. His hand was steady as he punched the numbers to Camp 22's director.

"This is General Sin Jai-Bong. It seems we have a situation here in Chongjin."

***

As soon as she heard someone approaching, Hannah stopped humming to herself. So-Young peeked in through the crack in the door. "I'm sorry to bother you." Hannah could barely hear her words. "My father wishes to speak with you. Do you need help getting up?"

Hannah shook her head. Her leg had been growing stronger with each week she spent in Mr. Kim's safe house. Her gait was still slow, but she could move around now with only the slightest trace of a limp. Her other wounds from Chongjin had scarred over and usually only bothered her at night. She had grown to hate the darkness and would have asked Mr. Kim for an extra candle if she didn't fear he'd scoff at the extravagance of her request.

She slid out of bed, holding her breath when she put her weight on her injured leg. So-Young made a move to come in, but Hannah held up her hand. She didn't need assistance, not for something as simple as walking. She made her way to the living room, where Mr. Kim sat with a book open on his lap.

"Take a seat," he mumbled without looking up.

So-Young floated soundlessly out of the room. Hannah watched her leave with the first pangs of trepidation gnawing inside her belly. Ever since she arrived at the safe house, she had rehearsed Mr. Kim's rules to herself several times a day. She even tried to obey the impossible ones, like his edict against listening to conversations with outsiders. The walls just weren't thick enough. Mr. Kim frowned, but she was used to his severe expression by now.

"Your leg is healed." He placed his book on the table between them.

"Yes, sir."

She was about to mention how helpful So-Young had been when he continued, "You realize that you were saved from the Chongjin jail for a specific purpose."

She nodded. She replayed her last minutes in Chongjin with tortuous regularity, trying to understand why she was sent here while Simon was left behind.

"There are some leaders of the North Korean church who believe you are an asset to their cause," Mr. Kim stated. "Have you heard of a man named Moses?"

She paused. She had heard of him on more than one occasion at the safe house, but never out in the open. Her pulse quickened, and she was thankful he didn't give her time to answer.

"Moses is a pillar. If it were not blasphemous to say so, I would go so far as to call him the cornerstone of the North Korean church. His influence stretches all the way from this side of the border to Pyongyang itself."

She didn't know what to say. She never heard Mr. Kim speak so reverently about anybody. She thought about Simon, about the plans he had for his ministry. He had never said so in words, but she understood by his prayers, by his body language, by his shining eyes whenever he talked about the underground church, that he held lofty ambitions. Had he heard of Moses before? Had he hoped to one day achieve such success for the kingdom of God? She didn't realize she had lost the flow of the conversation until Mr. Kim cleared his throat impatiently. She glanced around, as if the room itself might hint at what she should say next.

"Yes, sir," she answered and felt the warmth creeping up to her cheeks.

"You're not afraid, then?" Mr. Kim leaned toward Hannah. For the first time in her entire stay at the safe house, he looked directly into her eyes. Her lip trembled, but she shook her head without diverting her gaze.

"Good," he declared. "Be ready tomorrow."

She hoped he didn't hear her suck in her breath. She bit her bottom lip. "Tomorrow?" She racked her brain to try to catch the words she missed while daydreaming.

"Yes." Mr. Kim stood up and adjusted his shirt. "Moses wants to interview you. He'll be here a few hours before sunrise."

CHAPTER 17

Hannah had trouble sleeping even on normal nights. There was no way she could rest now. Thoughts and questions raced through her mind, each vying for her focus, warring for her attention. Who was this Moses, and what did he want with her? If he had been involved in her rescue from Chongjin, could she convince him to help Simon as well?

The front door of the safe house creaked open, even though the sun had set hours ago. Hannah heard its groaning hinges, and hundreds of tingles pranced up and down her back. Was Moses already here? She drew the covers up to her chin and waited. Mr. Kim's firm footsteps sounded near the entryway.

"Good evening, Uncle." At the sound of Kwan's voice, Hannah released her hold on the quilt. At least it was someone she knew. But what had Mr. Kim meant when he mentioned an interview? The only interviews Hannah knew of were the kind that took place behind locked doors of interrogation rooms. Surely Moses didn't intend to harm her. And if he did, Mr. Kim would never allow it.

Would he?

Mr. Kim grunted a greeting. Hannah heard the scuffle of chairs as he and Kwan took their seats in the kitchen. She pictured Kwan warming his hands in the steam from Mr. Kim's bitter tea, and she shivered with cold. There was already a light covering of snow on the mountains. She often wondered how Simon was faring wherever he was, and she prayed for a mild winter.

"When will he be meeting with her?"

"Tomorrow." Hannah often wondered how So-Young had developed such a gracious manner of speaking when her father's style was so brusque.

It took a while for Kwan to respond. "Where's the interview?"

"Up the mountain. Hermit's cabin."

"What time?"

"Early."

Their volume decreased. Hannah rolled onto her side and thought about the beloved resting her head on her lover's shoulder in the Song of Solomon. She hummed softly to herself, trying not to eavesdrop, but patches of the conversation still drifted through to her. *Take her myself ... still injured, you know ... slow you down.*

She stayed awake long after the voices ceased.

***

"There's a new believer here. He's met Moses."

At this declaration, the usual calm of the underground meeting vanished. Disregarding the usual appeal for deliberation and prayer before inviting new guests, the men reached up and nearly dragged the wide-eyed new arrival down the ladder. Before he even sat down, they barraged him with a cacophony of questions.

"Does Moses know about the believers here?"

"Has he said anything about Camp 22?"

"Is he in good health?"

"Is there a way to ask him to send a message to my sister?"

"Can he get us a Bible, do you suppose?"

Mal-Chin had to raise his whisper to a forceful hiss to calm the group down. "Give the kid some space." The prisoners reluctantly stepped back. "That's better." Mal-Chin turned to the newcomer. "So it's true that you've met Moses?"

The boy swallowed hard, and the sound of his constricting

throat carried through the silence. "Once."

That single word invited a new wave of interrogations.

"How old is he?"

"Did he mention who he works with?"

"What are his connections in Pyongyang?"

It was several minutes before Mal-Chin and the overseer finally quieted everyone back down, and that only succeeded after they threatened to disband the meeting. Once everyone was seated, Mal-Chin beckoned to the guest. "If we promise to listen calmly, will you tell us what you know?"

Simon saw the prisoner's lower jaw quiver ever so slightly. "I met Moses about two years ago." Everyone instinctively leaned forward. "It was across the border, at a safe house there."

"Where was the safe house?" another man asked. "What town?" A nudge from Mal-Chin silenced him.

The newcomer took a shaky breath before he continued. "I was like you. I had heard legends about him. When I got the chance to meet him, I was terrified. Scared he wouldn't be everything I thought he was." He paused and stared hard at the men surrounding him. "But he was. And even more."

"How does he cross the border so many times without getting caught, do you think?"

"How often does he visit Pyongyang?"

"When does he expect we'll all be free?"

Simon asked as many questions as the others, and even Mal-Chin joined in with a few of his own. It grew obvious there would be no more reasonable discussion, so the men dispersed with plans to meet again in four nights. Simon noticed the unusual lightness in Mal-Chin's step as they returned to the mass of sleeping prisoners, but he only felt tired. So Moses wasn't just a myth, but what good would that do tomorrow when Simon took his blistered hands and shoveled coal all day long? Would eyewitness proof of Moses' existence bring him one step closer to seeing Hannah again before the National Security Agency killed them both?

He stayed awake long after Mal-Chin's contented snores joined in with all the other nighttime sounds in the Camp 22 dorm.

CHAPTER 18

She heard muffled sounds outside her bedroom door and sat up, trying to remember if she had actually fallen asleep or not. It was before dawn. The chickens weren't even ready to awaken the world with their clucking. Hannah hadn't bothered to undress the night before, so she stepped out of bed, straightened her blouse, and tiptoed to the door. She couldn't decide if she should wait for Mr. Kim to summon her or just go out there, so she paused at the threshold, waiting in the dark.

"She still favors her leg when walking," Mr. Kim was saying.

"She'll need to go slow." It was Kwan's voice. Had he spent the night at the safe house, then? A soft tapping made Hannah take a quick step back. "Are you awake?" Kwan whispered. She paused for a moment so nobody could tell she had been standing there already and then opened the door. Kwan studied her face with concern and glanced down at her leg. "Did you get some rest? It's going to be a long way."

Mr. Kim had his back to her and was filling a small sack with rolls. He held the package out to Kwan. "Make sure she wears a coat."

"Are you ready?" Kwan held up the bag. "We'll eat our breakfast on the way."

Until now, Hannah had assumed Mr. Kim would escort her. She tried to hide her surprise. "I think so. I just need ..." She eyed the back door.

Kwan shuffled his feet. "I'll meet you outside in a minute."

Hannah put on her shoes and made her way to the outhouse.

Her leg was stiff but not terribly sore yet. She wondered how long their hike would take. Most of all, she wondered what kind of man was waiting for her at the end of their journey.

Kwan avoided her gaze when she came out the outhouse. They fell into a plodding rhythm which wasn't exactly easy, but at least Hannah could keep up. "So you've known Mr. Kim for a while?" she asked once she grew accustomed to the pace.

"You could say that."

She noticed the way his shoulders tensed up at the question, and she tried to find another subject. "What exactly is it that Moses does?"

Kwan chuckled while holding a branch back to allow her to pass by. "A better question is what he *doesn't* do." She hoped that wasn't the only answer she was going to get. After another moment, he continued, "He's known for lots of things, depending on who you ask. Smuggling Bibles. He's got important contacts in Pyongyang. If a Christian leader's about to be arrested, he sneaks them over the border. A few times, he's even managed to free someone condemned to execution."

She immediately thought of Simon. "How's he manage that?"

Kwan mopped his brow. "Those aren't the kind of questions you ask."

She kept her mouth shut. The early sun lit up the sky in a brilliant display of more orange and red tones than she could name. The forest floor was mushy, and the earthy scent of decaying leaves wafted around them. Hannah felt her ankle swelling up slightly, but Kwan was considerate enough to stay slow. She was sure he could bound up the mountain in a fraction of the time it was taking her.

As they walked on, they passed dry streambeds filled with dead leaves, and Hannah thought about the fall day over a year ago when she first arrived at the Sterns'. She had come to Yanji searching for Woong, the flower-swallow from the streets who had disappeared one night while she slept. As her hunt led only to greater disappointment and brought her closer to starvation, she eventually stopped looking for him and focused on her own survival. She wasn't experienced, not like the Yanji girls parading around in miniskirts, but she knew enough to understand her safety was at risk if she didn't find shelter soon.

Hannah's arrival at the Sterns' was nothing less than divine providence. Three Chinese pastors had turned her away before one Korean-speaking minister told her about the couple living on the outskirts of the city limits. "They are American. They have less to lose if they are caught by the police." With apologies for not being able to help her directly, the pastor gave her directions to the Sterns' home.

Hannah closed her eyes for a moment and breathed in the thin, crisp air. The chill pricked at her lungs, and when she exhaled, her breath came out in a cloudy fog. She thought about everything she had experienced since last fall and wondered how a life could change so drastically in a single year.

Kwan stopped on the trail in front of her and shuffled his feet in the dirt.

"Are we almost there?" she asked hopefully.

Kwan squirmed and glanced at his hands. "I'm ... I'm sorry. We need to ..." He looked around from one side of the woods to the other. Why was he acting so nervous? Had somebody followed them? He cracked his knuckles, and she winced involuntarily. "You see ..." The cold air forced miniature tears to the corners of her eyes. They were too small to blink away. He reached deep into his pocket. The black cloth he pulled out hung limp in his hand. "You need to put this on." The words that followed were so mumbled she wasn't certain what they were, but she guessed by his body language he was apologizing again.

She reached out for the cloth. It was a mask of sorts that covered the entire face, but the two slits that would have allowed her to see were sewn shut with thick white thread. "You want me to wear this?"

Kwan didn't raise his eyes from the forest floor.

For the first time, she wished she had told Mr. Kim she wasn't ready to get involved in underground ministry again. She was too young. Her leg wasn't fully healed. And her time in Chongjin ... Hannah had enough nightmares. She didn't want to go back. She'd find another way to help her compatriots. She'd speak in South Korean churches about the need for more Bibles or go back to the Sterns' and help refugees in Yanji. Her hand trembled as she put the mask over her face. Each time she breathed, tiny beads of cotton threatened to lodge in her lungs. She had no idea what she was doing, but she wasn't ready for it. She probably would never be ready. She remembered the darkness of her jail cell in Chongjin, and her body quivered against her will. Her ankle throbbed, and she couldn't take a full breath without breathing in lint.

Kwan pressed his hand into the small of her back. "Are you ready?"

At first, Hannah couldn't decide if it was more bearable to keep her eyes open or shut in the crude mask. She blinked once and coughed, the steam from her breath warming her entire face. "I'm ready." It was the first time she lied since leaving Chongjin.

Tears of humiliation stung her eyes when Kwan took her hand to lead her farther up the trail. Would God really lead her now to a ministry apart from Simon, call her to a life of service while Simon languished in prison camp or some jail cell? If only she imprisoned with him. If only they were together to share some encouragement, some support. What wouldn't she do for the chance to sing just one more hymn together? She missed the strong sound of his voice, his soothing laughter, his calm and quiet responses to all her questions about faith and the Bible. She didn't want to be here, out in the open, the birds chirping, the air cool and refreshing.

She didn't want to be here with another man, a man who didn't know her past, who didn't understand her like Simon did. She hated questioning God's perfect plans, but the ache inside her swelled like a consuming flame as Kwan cleared his throat and made that horrible popping sound with his fingers.

"We're here."

She expected him to remove the blindfold so she could meet her interviewer face to face, but he just told her to duck slightly. He positioned a chair beneath her, and she realized the mask was to remain. The breeze was gone; they were indoors, but it was just as cold as it had been outside. The air felt heavy, and it was filled with a strange electricity Hannah didn't recognize. She took a breath to steady herself, but some more fuzz from the mask caught in her nostrils.

"I'll see you when you're done." Kwan touched her gently on the elbow.

Hannah sat up straight. "You're leaving?"

"It's for your own safety." She heard the snapping of his finger joints and the receding steps of his shoes, and before long, even those sounds were gone.

She shut her eyes, which somehow made her feel like she could control the darkness around her. She stretched her arms out just a little to see if she could learn anything about her surroundings. The breeze flapped past. She longed for a breath of fresh air and wondered if someone could actually suffocate in this kind of mask. For a moment, she feared the entire meeting was a set-up. What if Moses wasn't really coming? What if it was a member of the Chinese police force, ready to take her back to North Korea? She'd be at the Chongjin jail by evening.

Her mind raced in a jumble of directions, with thoughts and fears flying haphazardly through her brain. She sat on her hands and tried counting slowly in her head. *One ... Two ...* If nothing happened by the time she reached ten, she would tear the mask off, regardless of the consequences.

Three ... Four ...

"You must be Hannah." The sound nearly made her fall out of her seat. She had no idea how large of a room she was in, but she felt the walls shrinking all around her. The stranger's voice was smooth, almost silky. "You have had a long journey, little warrior."

The diminutive drained the blood from Hannah's brain. The steamed roll she had eaten along the path sat like a stone in her gut, and she had to focus all her mental powers to keep it down where it belonged. A hand was on her shoulder, a hand that communicated both danger and power. Her instinct was to pull away, but her body refused.

"I apologize for such primitive hospitality."

Hannah's ankle ached. Her mouth was dry, and she was acutely aware of her chest rising and falling. If only she could lift the mask up and breathe normally. His fingers ran across her chin, and she sensed his hand was strong enough to snap her neck right there if he wanted her dead.

"There now," he crooned and lifted the mask just above her nose. The smell of rotting compost battled against the hint of strange cologne.

Hannah didn't realize her hands were clenched to the bottom of her chair until her shoulders protested from the tension. Her mouth was free, but her voice was gone. She may as well have left it back at the safe house in Sanhe.

"Is that better?"

Her body responded to the softness of his voice by relaxing. "Thank you." The words were out of her mouth before she even thought them. She still couldn't see anything through the sewn-up eyeholes, but she felt his smile on her, and she was no longer nauseated. Tentatively, she took a few deep breaths until her dizzy spell subsided.

"Now." That one word, spoken alone as if it were a statement of extreme significance, revealed the authority of its speaker, and Hannah's body leaned forward slightly. She had never heard such raw power so densely packed into a single syllable.

"I understand you made a big impact in Chongjin. Not many girls your age could have kept silent through so much."

She didn't want to think about Chongjin. "I was only trying to protect the mission." She couldn't explain why she felt like she had somehow just betrayed Simon.

Moses' voice contained the hint of a grin, but his words were drawn out so they sounded long and serious. "Yes, your mission. I'm very curious about the training you received at the Sterns'."

Hannah's spine straightened, just a small jolt she hoped he didn't observe. She leafed through the annals of her memory. Had she ever mentioned the Sterns by name to Mr. Kim or Kwan or anyone else? The dizziness returned in full force, and she pressed against her temples in protest.

Moses either didn't notice or didn't acknowledge her change in demeanor. "So, you were one of those sent out from this so-called 'Secret Seminary.' Am I correct?"

Thirsty. Hannah was thirsty. She opened her mouth once or twice but failed to produce any sound. A moment later, a hand caressed the back of her head, cradling her cranium, and a cool bottle was lifted gently to her lips. The liquid slipped down her throat. A tiny dribble spilled on her chin, and Moses wiped it away with the corner of his sleeve, making a kind of clucking sound like a mother might make over her sick child. His finger brushed against her cheek for a fraction of a second, and Hannah remembered the way she used to tuck the street children in with tattered rags or discarded blankets.

"I apologize." Moses' voice filled the room. "You have had a long journey. You're tired. This meeting must cause you a great deal of stress ... the mask and the secrecy. Forgive me. I'm not

..." Moses faltered, and Hannah couldn't tell if it was for effect or if he truly was baffled. "I'm not used to dealing with people like you." Hannah frowned, and Moses stumbled over his next words several times as if he were an awkward schoolboy. "You're young, you see. Not that you haven't endured a lifetime of trials already. It's just that ..."

"I understand," Hannah interjected, not because she truly did, but because she felt sorry for him while he faltered. "It's all right."

A blanket of warmth descended in the room, and a slight breeze carried the scent of pine. Moses laughed, not a hearty belly laugh, but a quiet, calming sort of chuckle that chased away the sharp prickles and nagging doubts that had oppressed Hannah since the beginning of their interview.

"You are a remarkable young woman."

Hannah blushed and didn't even care if he noticed or not. She couldn't even guess how long the interview lasted. When it was over, Moses took her gently by the elbow and led her outside. He told her to wait for Kwan, reminded her not to remove the blindfold, and assured her that he held her in the highest esteem. She thought back on their conversation and couldn't have said if they had spent twenty minutes or several hours together.

Shortly after Moses took his leave, Kwan returned. "Are you all right?" he asked.

She nodded, blinking when he took off the mask. The sun glared overhead. She shielded her eyes, and they started their silent trek back down the mountain. Their descent was even slower than their hike up, and Hannah had to stop to rest her leg every ten minutes or so. Kwan treated her with great respect and patience, but she felt her spirit reaching back toward Moses. She thought about the Christian men who had influenced her in the past — Mr. Stern with his foreign accent and his emphasis on theology and book learning, Simon and his fiercely loyal and steadfast spirit. None of her past encounters had prepared her for someone like Moses.

When he spoke to her, his words flowed like the Tumen River with the first melting of the snow — powerful, captivating, unyielding. There was also a hint of wildness, a suggestion of danger she couldn't quite explain. She wondered if this was what the New Testament writers meant when they said Jesus spoke to the crowds as one with great authority.

Even with her mask off, she was silent for most of the return hike and couldn't decide if she felt more somber or emboldened from Moses' interview. It certainly wasn't what she had expected. It started out so formal, so calculating. There was an almost haughty aloofness about him that came out more in his presence than in his words or tone. And then, as fast as a summer storm vanishes after drenching everything in its path, all that changed. She couldn't exactly remember how or when the atmosphere transformed, but the results were dramatic. Moses knew of the Sterns, and she found such sweet release to be able to talk to someone about her time in the Secret Seminary. He even asked about Simon, and Hannah's body trembled as she freed her memories. She told Moses everything, everything except about how Simon broke down under the weight of interrogation. She recounted the way he found her in the woods, the peace she felt when they were together, and Moses spoke of Simon as if he also knew him and loved him deeply. Other times, he seemed content just to listen. He was so good at that, so good at drawing out the words Hannah's soul needed to communicate to somebody, anybody who would understand.

As they walked down the mountain trail, Kwan glanced behind at Hannah every once in a while. She was afraid he was going to ask her a question and break the peaceful, blissful calm that had overcome her soul. She let the fresh air fill her lungs until she was certain they would burst from fullness. She replayed in her mind all the instructions Moses gave her for her first mission. She was ready.

And this time, she wouldn't fail.

***

"Hey, where's that boy?"

"Yeah, I thought he was coming back to tell us more about Moses."

In the flickering lamplight, Simon saw the overseer glance anxiously at Mal-Chin. "Who was supposed to wake the new kid up?"

"I tried to find him before bed, but I couldn't."

The overseer turned to the other prisoners and scowled. "Anybody see him?"

Nobody answered. Men fidgeted in their seats, and one scooted farther into the shadows.

"Was he at work in the mines today?" Several faces turned pale. Simon glanced at the ladder. "I told you we shouldn't just let anyone in," the overseer hissed at Mal-Chin.

One of the prisoners jumped up, but Mal-Chin blocked his path, folding his arms across his massive chest. "Where do you think you're going?"

The prisoner tried to swing a leg over the ladder. "What if we've been set up?"

Mal-Chin pulled him down by the back of his shirt as easily as if he had been a mere child. "Maybe we have. But how is stampeding out of here like a herd of wild animals supposed to help?"

Simon's temple throbbed, pulses of pain prophesying his doom in the darkness. Mal-Chin laid a hand on the prisoner's shoulder. "There's nothing to do about it, Brother. Maybe we were wrong to let him in. Maybe he was just a plant from the camp guards to get us to talk, but we don't know that. Not yet. I say we start our Bible study. Brother Simon, are you ready to teach us more from the Sermon on the Mount? I suggest we all practice the passage about worry. And those of you who don't want to stay, well, you can leave one at a time every five minutes. Calm and orderly."

Simon unclenched his jaw. Several of the other men relaxed, and a few moved closer to the ladder. Simon thought about the passage they were about to recite when a shout cracked through the silence like the burst of a gun. His body went perfectly rigid, his mind momentarily blank as a white light from the entrance above blinded his eyes.

"They're down here." At the sound of their own condemnation, a few men scurried as far back as possible. One ducked down and covered his head. The rest, like Simon, froze in place. Boots stomped on the rungs. Half a dozen flashlight beams sliced through the darkness like knife blades. An old man began to cry, and another prisoner recited the Lord's Prayer in a frantic hush.

A man in front of Simon shrieked, "Protect us, Jesus. Save us from these men. Have mercy ..." His prayer was silenced in one loud, deafening flash followed by the stench of burning sulfur.

Mal-Chin took a step toward the guards. "Welcome, gentlemen. We weren't expecting you."

"Shut up, granddad." One of the agents cracked Mal-Chin's skull open with the butt of his revolver. The old man's body crumpled without a sound, like a coat blown off its hanger. The puddle of blood beneath him widened, the deep red a striking contrast to the olive-green of the officers' uniforms. Someone yanked Simon up by the collar and bound his wrists behind his back. The cords cut into his skin, but he didn't fight back. His only thought was that his blood would soon match Mal-Chin's, who now lay in a lifeless heap at the base of the ladder.

***

Moses adjusted the collar of his shirt and scratched at the stubble on his chin. He had never relied on someone that young before. He had very little doubt the new girl was brave, but her age alone was a strong disadvantage. Absorbed in brooding thoughts, he made his way down the mountain and toward the Tumen River. Mr. Kim thought highly enough of her abilities, but even the old safe-house director didn't quite understand the kind of mission she was expected to fulfill.

Moses had long since given up sleeping more than three or four hours a night, and he let the cool morning air clear his mind. He needed to be alert. He still had a full day of work ahead of him.

Fording the frigid Tumen River was no problem at all. He could probably make the journey blindfolded. Even if he were caught, he knew exactly how to avoid trouble. He never crossed the border without his paperwork in impeccable order. A few minutes later, he arrived at his van. He got in, slammed the door, and put his boots back on over his wet feet. Revving up the engine, he wondered for the smallest moment if recruiting the girl was the right decision. Then he rolled down his window so the icy breeze would keep him focused and sharp. His pager beeped once, and Moses glanced at it without slowing down. When he read the message, he frowned and pulled out his large radio from the glove box.

"I'm coming in right now."

PART 3

CHAPTER 19

The last time she had seen Agent Soon, he stood half naked on the bank of the Tumen River giving her directions to Sanhe. At that point, Hannah neither hoped nor expected to ever meet him again. Now, she made her way over with a timid smile.

He sighed audibly when she came up to him, his breath coming out like gray smoke. "I'm glad you arrived safely. Did you have any problems crossing?"

"No." The river was frozen now, and her leg had ample time to heal at Mr. Kim's safe house. It still ached, but she hardly even limped anymore.

"I was praying for your success."

Hannah sensed the admiration in Soon's tone. *The youngest railroad conductor.* That's what Moses called her when they met up on the mountaintop several months ago. She was now the youngest member of Moses' web of contacts who smuggled Christian leaders in and out of North Korea. Her job was to relay information only, but that information would play a pivotal role in keeping workers on both sides of the border in communication with one another.

"He didn't tell me it would be you," Hannah admitted. She was forbidden from speaking Moses' name, even here. The secrecy alone was exhilarating. For the first time since she left the Secret Seminary, she was part of something important, something destined to succeed. She still didn't know how the details she would collect from Soon could benefit the underground church in the end, but she knew this was a plan that would never fail. Being part of this group of spies and informants and secret workers made her heart race. Gone were the days of feeling broken and useless. Gone were the days of pining for things that must never be. This was her future. This was her calling.

Soon slipped her a small envelope, and she noticed he had a hard time meeting her gaze. She blamed the flush that crept up into her own face on the cold and nothing else. She was a real underground worker now, not a disheveled refugee trained by foreigners. She was a member in a network of dozens, perhaps even hundreds, of courageous heroes and heroines whose influence stretched from Pyongyang to Beijing. The people she worked for had even rescued Christian prisoners from jails and labor camps.

She lingered a moment longer. Moses hadn't given her any other instructions besides taking Soon's note to Mr. Kim. "Is there anything else you need?" she asked.

"Not tonight." Soon cleared his throat, and they stared at one another's feet. "Safe journey," he finally whispered.

Hannah scurried back over the frozen river.

***

After his meeting with the girl from Sanhe, Soon managed to arrive before dawn for his shift at the Chongjin jail, but General Sin was already waiting for him. "Get me that Christian prisoner we got transferred from Onsong last fall."

Soon's stomach dropped. Everything had gone so well this morning.

"Is there a problem?" the general probed.

Soon stammered a reply. "He's very sick, sir." He glanced around the room, as if it might give a hint how to change the general's mind. Levi hadn't been questioned for months. Soon hoped General Sin was done interrogating him. "He's not well at all."

"Then hurry up and fetch him before he gets worse," the general snapped. Soon was dismissed. He sulked downstairs.

"I've told you everything," Levi whispered once Soon entered his cell. His choked voice made him sound old enough to be Soon's grandfather, even though he was still a young man.

"I know." Soon kept his voice low so other co-workers wouldn't hear. "You've done well. The general just wants to talk to you again."

"I've told you everything. Everything." Levi's body heaved. His sharp shoulder blades poked into Soon's chest as he helped the prisoner to his feet. "I don't know anything else." Levi was sobbing.

Soon steeled himself against the stench of infected flesh, hoping the prisoner didn't notice him gag. Levi's cheekbones were so caved in Soon could have filled them both with water, and none would spill out. Levi stumbled, and Soon pictured how easy it would be to scoop him up like an infant and carry him all the way to the interrogation room. He gritted his teeth against the odor and wondered how much longer he'd have to stay here in Chongjin. The best he could hope for was a ticket across the border before things got too awful. Second to that was a quick and painless death. He had witnessed far too many of the other kind.

Levi lost his footing, and Soon scraped a huge scab off the prisoner's arm while trying to catch him. Levi cried out but sounded more like a frog or a toad than a human. When he first arrived in Chongjin, Levi sang hymns all through the night. He had a beautiful voice, but that was before General Sin got to him.

"We're almost there," Soon whispered. "Please. Please let me help you just a little bit farther."

Levi tensed his muscles. Soon felt like he should offer the prisoner some form of comfort before his meeting with the general. He swung open the heavy door of the interview room, his stomach somersaulting. He gave the countertops a cursory glance to make sure they were clean enough for General Sin's expectations and led Levi to the chair. He patted him once on the shoulder but didn't strap him in. Tears leaked out of the prisoner's eyes.

"Good luck, Brother."

Soon doubted Levi even heard.

***

As soon as he entered the interrogation room, General Sin dismissed Soon and flicked his cigarette onto the floor near the prisoner's feet. "Do you know why I brought you here?"

Soundless sobs scrunched up the boy's face. He shook his head.

"I brought you here," the general stated, "because you insisted that Moses was more than a myth."

Levi shut his eyes and held up his fingers as if in protest. "I signed the statement. I gave the confession."

Sin clucked his tongue. "But you didn't believe it, did you?" he hissed directly into the prisoner's ear. "You know there really is a Moses, and you were trying to find him, weren't you?"

Levi's body shook. Nothing grated on the general's nerves like the sound of rattling teeth. "I ... I don't know what you want me to say."

The general clucked his tongue once more. "It's no matter, anyway." He flicked his wrist as if he were swatting away a pesky fly. "You and I both know the truth. Unfortunately, for some people here, that's a problem."

Levi kept his eyes scrunched up, leaving only the smallest of slits open.

General Sin could only imagine what it would be like to come directly under the white lights of the interview room after spending weeks in darkness and isolation. "You know I'm doing you a favor." Sin strode to the counter.

"No." Levi's voice was raspy, but the pleading filled the room. Sin filled up his syringe. "No," the prisoner whimpered. Sobs wracked his whole body. "No more drugs."

The general opened a vial. "I already told you. I'm doing you a favor."

Levi trembled. "For God's sake," he croaked, "have mercy. No more drugs."

Sin was at his shoulder now, his dose ready. With his free hand, he scrunched up Levi's sleeve. The prisoner was too weak to protest. Sin positioned his back to the room's surveillance camera and leaned in so close his beard stubble scratched against Levi's cheek. "That's what I'm doing," he whispered. "Having mercy."

Levi writhed, tensing his entire body. Sin plunged the needle into his arm and drained the colorless poison into his vein. Once the syringe was empty, he tossed it back onto the counter. Levi's face was already beginning to relax.

"It won't change anything, but you were right," Sin whispered before the prisoner lost complete consciousness. "You see, I am Moses."

Levi's eyes flickered shut.

CHAPTER 20

Hannah paused at the entry to the safe house just long enough to catch her breath. If Mr. Kim was awake, she didn't want to barge in with a silly grin on her face after her first delivery. The work Moses recruited her for was serious — deadly serious — and the last thing she wanted was for Mr. Kim to think she was too immature to pull it off.

She donned a neutral expression and creaked open the front door. Mr. Kim sat at the table reading by candlelight. He ignored the hissing tea kettle and didn't look up when she came in. She wanted to slip to her room and warm up under a big pile of blankets, but he stopped her. "You didn't get lost or anything?"

She paused just long enough to whisper a reply.

Mr. Kim tilted his chin slightly in acknowledgement. "Good."

It was the highest praise he had ever given her.

***

Soon leaned over the toilet. The strain from his retching brought tears to his eyes. He splattered water onto his face and wiped his mouth clean before flinging the bathroom door open and scurrying over to his superior's office. The general was smoking a cigarette, his feet on his desk. He didn't glance up when Soon stormed in. "I thought you'd come stopping by for a visit."

"I need to talk to you." Soon tried to keep his voice steady.

General Sin gestured to the surveillance camera with the flick of his wrist. "I know. Talk."

Soon glanced at the camera hidden in the corner.

"It's off," the general snapped.

"Won't that make them suspicious?"

"They know I have my reasons. Now what do you want?"

Soon begged his tears not to fall. "You killed him."

The general shrugged. "That way you didn't have to."

"He was loyal. He didn't deserve ..." Soon stopped. He doubted his voice.

General Sin swung his feet to the ground. "He didn't deserve a life behind bars. He's free now."

Free. Such a simple word. So impossible to attain in this God-forsaken land. Soon cleared his throat. "He ... he was a good man."

"Agreed." General Sin folded his hands on the desk. "Which is why I didn't send him to the gulag."

Soon swallowed away the lump in his throat. His body quivered, both with anger and terror. "You didn't send him to the gulag because you didn't want him spreading more rumors."

Sin narrowed his eyes but said nothing, so he went on.

"You talk about the cause. You prattle on about the work still left to do. And yet with your own two hands you kill innocent men, men a hundred times more honorable and more courageous than you could ever ... than you will ever ..." He wiped his eyes in frustration.

The eruption he expected never came. The general raised a single eyebrow and kept his hands folded in his lap. "Are you done?"

Soon turned his face away to hide his tears.

General Sin gestured toward the door. "If that's all you have to say, then I suggest you finish cleaning up the interrogation room."

***

Kwan stopped by that afternoon. Hannah couldn't tell if she was just imagining things or if he was really looking at her with increased respect and admiration. "I hear you made your first delivery this morning." Mr. Kim had gone out to tend to the chickens, and everyone else sat by the fire.

Hannah kept her hands clasped in her lap and nodded.

"Did your leg give you any trouble?"

She wasn't sure where to focus her eyes. It felt vain to meet his. She ended up staring at the top button on his shirt and shook her head.

Kwan stretched out his legs. "I remember my first donkey trip. I only carried three Bibles, but it felt like three truck loads. I was trembling so hard I'm surprised I ever found my way back."

She giggled, glad to shift the conversation away from herself. "Did you ever get caught?"

So-Young poked at the fire and sat down across from them without saying a word. Kwan sat up a little taller. "Well, there was one time …"

A cold burst of air blasted through the back door as Mr. Kim came in. "You'd better be on your way, Nephew. It will be getting dark soon."

***

Burying a prisoner had never taken Soon so long before. The heavy weight in his stomach seeped into his limbs, dragging him down. When he was finished, he crouched in the dirt, where one day his own body would meet its resting place. There were days he wished he never learned men were created for freedom and dignity. There were days he cursed his own conversion and the constant danger it forced upon him. He leaned over the makeshift grave, trying to fathom what type of prayer was appropriate for a travesty like this.

He knew it was General Sin behind him by the way the dirt trembled under the forceful strides. Soon didn't turn around. The general had already seen his tears once.

"You did well today." General Sin never offered praise before. Soon lifted his finger to his cheek and pretended to scratch it. He made a move to stand up, but General Sin squatted down next to him. For a moment, the two kept silent vigil before Levi's unmarked grave. Soon could hear the general's throat working each time he swallowed. Finally, the general coughed and mumbled, "For the kingdom to advance, we must all be prepared to make sacrifices."

A dozen questions hung on Soon's shoulders like chinks in an iron chain until he finally found his courage and his voice. "When you say 'sacrifices,' do you mean martyrdom? Or murder?"

General Sin picked up a stick and etched lines in the dirt. "Yes."

Soon didn't ask any other questions.

CHAPTER 21

Hannah crossed the border several more times over the next few weeks. Even though the subsequent trips were never quite as invigorating as her first, she was glad for the chance to feel useful. Now that her leg was mostly healed, she could think of no better way to serve her countrymen. Of course, she didn't know what kind of messages she was relaying between the safe house and Agent Soon, but Moses had assured her the work was critically important.

Whenever exhaustion from her sleepless nights dragged her down, she thought of Moses. When frightening sounds startled her in the darkness, she wished for another chance to meet him just to glean some more of his conviction and strength. Would he be proud of the work she was doing? Would he be surprised someone her age had made so many successful deliveries? Sometimes she imagined he was watching her, hiding behind some tree stump or crouching just around the corner of the trail. If she were caught or attacked, he would be ready to protect her.

"Have you ever met him?" she asked Soon one cold and starlit night. She needed to return home before it got any later, but she had been trying to gather up the courage to ask Soon about Moses for weeks.

He glanced over his shoulder and lowered his voice. "Who?"

"You know."

"Him?"

She nodded.

"No."

They both looked down, neither one willing to break the ensuing silence. It was time for Hannah to go. She turned back to the river.

"He's at Camp 22, you know."

She spun around.

Soon rubbed his hands together in the cold. "Your friend. He's at Camp 22. I saw the transfer orders myself." His countenance fell when she met his gaze. "I thought you'd be happy to know. He's safe now. I mean ..." He looked at her, his face searching, almost pleading with hers. Finally, he bowed his head. "I'm sorry. I just wanted to tell you he was still alive. I think ... I think he would have wanted you to know."

Hannah went on without saying anything. She was still numb with cold hours after returning to the safe house. Hot tea, layers of blankets, nothing offered any warmth. The tears she expected to shed never fell. Soon hadn't told her anything her heart didn't already know, and her tears had dried up long ago.

***

As soon as he finished his work for the day, Soon headed toward the grave of the fallen missionary. Staring at the lump of dirt, now covered with frost, Soon wondered yet again what he was still doing in Chongjin. He thought about Hannah, the sweet girl who passed him messages from the safe house in Sanhe, and the young man who had been captured at the same time. Soon thought about his own comrades. Would anybody cry for him if he were taken to prison camp?

Soon bowed his head over the grave. "I'm sorry." He wondered if such crimes as his could merit forgiveness.

"You know, he doesn't care if any of us visit his grave or not." Soon couldn't imagine a more unwelcome sound. He acknowledged the general with a small nod but said nothing. "You wonder if there was something else you could have done to keep him alive," General Sin stated, bringing an unexpected lump to the back of Soon's throat. He clenched his fists. He wouldn't let the general manipulate his emotions. "You're hardly sleeping at night," Sin continued, "and you've all but stopped praying because you don't think you're worthy anymore to present your requests to the Almighty. Am I right?"

Soon let his head drop once in affirmation.

The general took a step forward and clasped his hands behind his back. "Now you know how I feel." Soon cocked his head. Was the general mocking him? "Even now," General Sin continued, "I ask myself if it's really worth it. Am I really making a difference in the end? And do you know what I figured?"

"What?" The word croaked out of Soon's mouth before he could stop it. He stared at the makeshift grave of a man who should have been his friend. His brother.

General Sin coughed once before responding. "I figured I'm a dead man either way. So I may as well try to make something of a difference before the inevitable."

Soon struggled to keep his voice calm. "You call this making a difference?" He gestured to the undignified mound of dirt. "This isn't the way to do it. This isn't the way to change lives."

The general laughed mirthlessly. "You sound just like your missionary friend." He waved his hand at the grave. "I suppose you'll tell me that he's the one who fulfilled his heavenly calling, while I've done nothing but hinder the kingdom. That's what you really think, isn't it?"

Soon didn't have a ready answer.

"Because, let me remind you," Sin went on, "about that little Christian girl you've been meeting. What do you suppose would have happened if I hadn't let her go? Do you care to guess where she'd be right now?"

Soon cringed and shook his head.

"Or should I tell you about all the cases you've never even heard of? The prisoners who wet my feet with their tears, crying for joy when I bring them to safety. Should I tell you about them? The mothers I reunite with their children. The men who go back to smuggling Bibles because I look the other way when processing their intake papers. The pastor who receives an anonymous warning about a raid that would cost his life and send his pregnant wife to hard labor. You pick, Agent Soon. Tell me which story you want to hear next. And then decide who is and who isn't advancing the kingdom."

Soon winced. He didn't have the strength to meet his superior's gaze.

"That's what I thought." General Sin spat on the dirt and walked away.

***

A very soft snow fell outside, muffling the noise of the outside world. The fire crackled while Hannah helped So-Young wash the dinner dishes.

"Will you be crossing the river again sometime soon?" So-Young asked, passing Hannah a small plate.

"Not until the snow stops. It's too easy to track like this."

"It must be nice," So-Young whispered.

"What?"

"Getting out."

Hannah glanced around for Mr. Kim.

"Kwan says the other side of the border is a lot like Sanhe. Just poorer," So-Young breathed.

Hannah shouldn't say anything else. So-Young was still a child. She didn't need to worry about the oppression that robbed individuals of their humanity just a few kilometers away. "Kwan's right." Hannah tried to think of some way to change the subject.

"They say in North Korea parents are allowed to have as many children as they want."

Hannah thought of the countless flower-swallows she had cared for. Some were orphans, but the majority were simply abandoned when their parents grew too poor to feed them. For someone like So-Young, perhaps the idea of a large family with siblings running all around was pleasant.

"Kwan tells me the food is different too, that they're such good cooks they invented a way to turn tree bark into stew." So-Young giggled. "I wonder what it tastes like."

"It sounds like Kwan tells you lots of things about the outside world." Hannah didn't understand why So-Young grew so quiet, but the next few minutes passed by in awkward silence. "You're lucky to have such a good friend." Hannah rinsed her hands. "I can tell you and Kwan are very close."

"He's my best friend." So-Young's eyes beamed. "When I grow up, I think he might even become my fiancé." Her face grew pensive. "Did you have a fiancé in North Korea?"

Images raced through Hannah's mind in fast motion. Simon laughing with the other Secret Seminary students, Simon sitting next to her on the bench in Mrs. Stern's garden, Simon raising his voice in excitement as he expounded on a new revelation from the Scriptures.

"Well?" So-Young gave her a playful sideways glance. "Did you have a fiancé or not?"

Hannah wiped her hands dry on her apron. "No. No, I never had a fiancé."

CHAPTER 22

Day and night were meaningless distinctions in solitary confinement. Simon forgot how long it had been since he last saw another human being. At the Secret Seminary, Mr. Stern had prepared a crisis training program to equip the students for interrogations and torture. It hardly touched on the horror of total isolation.

And the silence. It made his ears physically hurt. At times, Simon was convinced he heard voices talking. Some hissed to one another in the darkness, teasing Simon's sleep away. Others were kinder, softer, but vanished as soon as he responded to them. At the Secret Seminary, he had been one of the quickest to memorize Bible passages, but here, with his body kept a few crumbs away from starvation, his mind tortured by the darkness and timelessness of his cell, it took ages to recite a simple verse. He was pretty sure that entire days went by when he couldn't recall even one passage from all of his studies. The most gruesome of his torments were his memories of Hannah. He could see her so vividly, sitting in Mrs. Stern's flower garden, the empty half of the bench beckoning to him with an intensity no living man should be forced to endure.

His crisis training in Yanji was designed to prepare him for pain. And although Mr. Stern mentioned the possibility of solitary confinement, Simon never really understood how horrendous it would be. He had assumed isolation would be easier than torture. How stupid he had been. The air in his cell was so heavy he could waste hours trying to pray without uttering a syllable. The same dark oppression that sucked his memory dry of Scripture pressed down on his soul. Sometimes it took every ounce of his spiritual stamina just to whisper the name of Jesus.

The hard cement floor and the constant hunger made it difficult to fall asleep, and what rest he did find was riddled with agonizing fears. He would wake up with a jerk, certain the guards were outside waiting to begin their torments. He was afraid to sleep because the darkness left him so disoriented. Had he been unconscious for a whole day or just a few hours? Sometimes he woke up in a horrid, damp sweat, certain he had squandered whole days of his life passed out on the cold floor.

His only solace was that he was here instead of Hannah. Maybe she had found a lenient job in one of the other labor camps. Maybe the Lord would hide her beauty from the lustful prison guards. Maybe her joyful spirit would sustain her through whatever suffering awaited her. Simon felt his own soul slipping away moment by elusive moment, but this hope for Hannah's future sustained him in that bleak, black purgatory. He might never see her again, but he would cherish her memory until his body finally gave out and his soul flew upward where his heavenly Father waited to receive him.

***

General Sin read the memo from the director of the National Security Agency, lit his cigarette, and read it again. There was no mistaking its message. The agency had linked Moses back to the Chongjin jail. Sin couldn't just deny it. Everyone in Pyongyang knew Moses was real, and they wanted him. Once they had him, they wouldn't stop until they extracted every ounce of information out of him. His mind wandered to desertion, but only for the briefest moment. He would never be safe, no matter what nation or embassy he found to take him in. He would never be free.

Sacrifices. That's what this masquerade was all about. Sacrifices for the good of the nation, for the good of the underground church. *Sacrifices.* Like that boy Levi from the Secret Seminary, the one buried out back. *Sacrifices.* The only currency worth anything in this clandestine world, where a clear conscience was an indulgence reserved only for cowards and a few fortunate fools.

Sacrifices.

Moses unlocked the bottom drawer of his desk, took out a small pill bottle, and pressed the button on his radio. "Get in here, Agent Soon. I need to talk with you."

***

Hannah knelt by her bed. It wasn't nighttime yet, but she was scheduled to meet with Soon later and wanted to spend some time in prayer. She was so tired. Her trips to the Tumen were sapping up what strength she had regained after leaving Chongjin. And even after she had been out all night making deliveries, Mr. Kim still expected her to wake up with the sunrise and see to breakfast and the chickens. By the end of the day, she was almost too tired to pray at all.

Back in Yanji, Mrs. Stern had taught her an entire prayer routine, starting with praise and thanksgiving, then moving on to confession and intercession. The ritual seemed stiff and formulaic, but Hannah figured Mrs. Stern must know what she was doing. The American missionary assured her it was the easiest, most foolproof way to keep from getting distracted.

Hannah had plenty to be thankful for, and she lifted her heart up to God who had healed her injuries from Chongjin and kept her safe on her journeys across the border. Throughout her entire life, God had protected her and provided for her, and now she was here, with a ministry and a purpose greater than she ever envisioned for herself. The Sterns hardly thought her ready to travel across the border with a meager supply of audio Bibles and New Testaments. Now she was part of a network that stretched all the way to Pyongyang. Her life was finally meaningful.

Or was it? Was she really doing what God called her to do? Or did she carry letters because Kwan and Moses and Mr. Kim and everyone else expected her to? Was she really an integral asset to Moses' team, or was she just one laborer amongst many, soon to be replaced when her luck ran out?

Her knees pressed against the hard floor, the discomfort reminding her she was supposed to be praying. She closed her eyes and thought about the sins she needed to confess. There was her general distractedness, of course. She found herself thinking more and more about Moses and the messages he wanted her to deliver. Surely she was doing the work of the Lord. Surely this excitement was from him. But the peace and contentment had vanished, replaced with a spirit of exhaustion. Back at the Secret Seminary, everything was so tranquil. Sitting on the garden bench and studying the Bible with Simon night after night, everything was so perfect, so complete.

Hannah wondered when she would ever find that sense of wholeness again.

***

Soon was filing paperwork when he got the summons from the general. What could it be now? Hadn't he already done enough? He forced himself to hurry down the hall. The general was waiting for him outside his office. "There's a problem out back." He gestured with a nod of his head. "Something wrong with the wiring. I need you to come with me."

They walked outside and stopped when they reached Levi's grave. General Sin's eyes were gray and expressionless. Soon had never seem him look so old. "They somehow connected Moses to the Chongjin jail." The general's voice was quiet and flat.

A quiver began in the base of Soon's gut. All his autonomic responses slowed down for a second and then sped ahead at full force. His mind raced even faster than his heartbeat, his thoughts expressing themselves in a jumble of impressions instead of actual words. "Hannah," he managed to stammer.

General Sin waved his hand, and Soon understood the sweet recruit from Sanhe was the least of his superior's worries. The general paced a few feet in either direction and rubbed his temples. There was a fleck of gray in the hair above his ears. "You have been loyal to me, Comrade." The general's tone was ominous. Soon glanced at him sideways. Was this a farewell? The general jerked his chin toward the grave. "I know you don't agree with my tactics."

Soon kept his eyes on the dirt.

"Just as well." General Sin shrugged. "But I hope you understand I care about you inasmuch as I am able." He reached into his pocket. "You may be questioned."

Soon stared at the small white pill but didn't reach out for it.

"One day, you might realize I was right. Some things are worse than the grave."

Tentatively, Soon took the capsule, surprised it didn't burn his skin on impact. It was so tiny, so delicate.

"If the time comes —" General Sin paused to clear his throat. "— I'm sure you will find courage to do the right thing."

Soon's lip trembled. He had so many questions vying for position on his tongue, but before he had time to ask any of them, General Sin turned away, suddenly looking bent over and very tired.

CHAPTER 23

General Sin's boots were as heavy as steel when he trudged up the small hill back to the jail. He brushed his hands on his uniform. A weaker man would question himself, and perhaps ten or fifteen years ago, Sin might have too. But he couldn't allow himself the extravagance of second guesses. There was only forward. There was only progress.

Progress and sacrifice.

He closed the door to his office, checking once to see if anyone had left him a message. He picked up his phone and dialed the number without any further hesitation.

"This is General Sin. I just discovered the connection between my jail and the convict Moses."

***

Soon's legs throbbed as he sprinted toward his meeting place with Hannah. He was half an hour early. *Please let her be there.* It had taken every ounce of fortitude in his body, but he had carried out his entire shift at the jail that day, and then he rushed home and packed his bag. He took the small amount of cash he had been saving for an emergency, thanked God he had no living family the regime could punish on his behalf, and hurried toward the Tumen.

His breath came out in short bursts. He forced himself to slow down. If someone saw him running this late at night, they'd get too curious. If Hannah wasn't there by the time he arrived, he'd cross alone and wait for her on the other side. They couldn't even stay in Sanhe, though. The guards would be after him as soon as they realized he escaped. If he was lucky, General Sin would wait a day or two before announcing his absence to the National Security Agency, but Soon couldn't be sure of even that. He had to leave now, and if Hannah wanted to stay safe, she'd come along with him.

The half-moon was out, and he felt the rush of relief warm his body when he saw Hannah's profile in the shadows ahead. He sprinted the last stretch and was out of breath by the time he reached her. He grabbed her arm. "Let's go."

"What's wrong?" Soon heard the catch in her voice, the fear he was certain laced all of his own words as well.

"They found us out. We've got to leave. For good."

He felt her arm tug back for just a second. "What about Simon?"

He dragged her forward. "You can't worry about him right now."

The moon gave off its brilliant light. Too much light. Soon wished he had a wristwatch. If General Sin called the National Security Agency from his office, they might have already beat them both here. The ice was slippery. He held onto Hannah to keep her from falling. They were going too slow. They had to reach the other side.

"Freeze!" The shout cracked like a whip through the air.

He gave Hannah a shove forward. "Hurry!" The momentum knocked him over. "Hurry," he hissed to her again until she started running. As he turned toward his assailants in their olive-green coats, he knew he'd never see the gentle girl from Sanhe again. His only hope was to distract the guards long enough to give her a head start.

He took in his surroundings in perfect panorama. Four men stood on the bank. Two pointed rifles at his head. Another held a dog that snarled as it strained against its leash. He couldn't hear

Hannah behind him anymore and hoped she made it to the other side. He squared his shoulders. There was no use running anymore. Somehow, he had always known it would happen this way. Tonight, or some other night just like it, Soon would face the Party members who wanted him dead. General Sin was right. If they caught him alive, Moses, Hannah, the Sanhe safe house — everything would be jeopardized. Soon slipped his hand into his pocket and fingered his pill. One of the men shouted a command to his dog and let go of the leash. The canine darted past Soon. He prayed it wouldn't reach Hannah.

"What are you doing there?" A guard dashed onto the ice but fell as soon as his boots hit the slippery surface. Soon had to act before it was too late.

"He put something in his mouth." The oldest agent reached him first, rammed his hand in Soon's mouth and tried to lodge it all the way down his throat. Soon scarcely heard him curse. Had Hannah made it to safety?

An instant later, the dog snarled just a little bit in the distance. Two of the men jogged onto the ice and hurried toward the direction of the sound. The other two lifted Soon between them. "Get him to the van. We'll pump his stomach."

Soon's vision started to blur. Didn't they know they couldn't touch him anymore? "We got the girl," someone called out, but he hardly heard them. He was safe forever, safe from their clutches, safe from their tortures. He shut his eyes. He spent his last prayer on Hannah, asking that God would send her angels to whisk her away to some secret refuge where the National Security Agency could never find her again.

Peace rushed through his body as his muscles locked up and his mouth frothed over.

A few short, painless seconds later, he was free.

**

General Sin scrawled notes on his clipboard while cigarette ash dropped on the page. He reached out mechanically for the phone when it rang. "Yes."

"We followed your agent. You were right. He was the link."

Sin tapped his pen against the receiver. "Thought so. Did you question him?"

There was a pregnant pause. "Unfortunately, he died before we had the chance."

Sin scowled and leaned forward in his chair.

The agent spoke fast, fumbling over his words. "There was a girl with him. Young. We have her now."

"Good." General Sin flicked cigarette ash over his metal tin and waited for more information.

"Should we bring her to you, sir?"

A note on the bottom of the page caught his attention, and he scribbled a few words in the margin. "Fine. Bring her in."

"Yes, sir."

He inhaled slowly. "On second thought, now Soon's gone, we're short on help. Take her to Camp 22. Let them see what she knows."

There was a slight pause before another "Yes, sir," and General Sin hung up the phone. He leaned back in his chair and resumed his paperwork. It would take at least another hour before he finished.

***

"Do you know where you are?"

Hannah shook her head. Throbbing pain pounded inside her skull. Pulsing white lights blinded her vision. Sticky blood caked onto her leg. She remembered the dog bite and shivered.

"You are in the underground detention center at Camp 22.

You are charged with selling state secrets and threatening national security."

Hannah struggled to keep her head up. The rest of her body was a pulp of bruises and brokenness, but all she felt was the anguish between her temples. A small cup was brought to her lips, and she lapped at the water clumsily.

"When you are strong enough, you will tell us who you were meeting. You will tell us about the traitor Soon and all those in your network of spies and conspirators." In spite of her weakness, she trembled violently. "You will cooperate."

The metal clanged into place as her cage door swung shut.

PART 4

CHAPTER 24

Simon knew winter had ended when his teeth stopped chattering at night. Sometimes he wondered if time had deceived him. Was it only a few months, or had he spent over a year in this black vacuum? Where was Hannah now? Was she even alive? He hated the thought of her trapped in a cell as dark and desperate as his.

Anxious fears collided against each other viciously, swirling chaotically in his soul. At first, he was optimistic his detainment would get easier. He'd grow accustomed to this timeless void. He'd establish a prayer routine and spend his days with purpose or at least some form of dignity. But as a humid spring chased away the harsh chill of winter, the despair only swelled and intensified. He stopped stretching his limbs or working his muscles. What was the point? He crouched uncomfortably day and night but lacked the energy or motivation to shift his position. He forced down all his fear into one small cavity of his chest, and he kept it cramped in there like a tiger confined in a cage two sizes too small.

He no longer questioned which voices were real and which were phantoms. When Hannah came to tend to him in his dreams, there was no longer any joy, even for the slightest moment. He knew all too soon he would wake up, never knowing if it was night or day, and she would desert him without a hint of farewell. On occasion, the guards came. They had to drag him down the hall, not because he struggled, but because he was too weak to walk on his own. He was always blindfolded, so he couldn't even see the other prisoners he passed. During the questionings, his body reacted to the pain, but his mind had long since fallen numb. When his accusers demanded information about other Christians in Camp 22, Simon told them nothing. He had already failed that test once. He had learned his lesson. Even the guards grew despondent and bored, and the interviews grew shorter and less violent.

Simon assumed one day the agents would go a little too far, or his body would give in to malnutrition or infection, and he would finally be released. There would be no other rescue. When his body gave way to fever and his breathing grew raspy and rattled, he guessed how many more days he had to wait, but even the prospect of heaven brought only a small trace of joy. With each breath, it felt like wasps were stinging him from the inside, and the simple act of breathing left him sweaty and depleted. All he wanted was rest. He was so very tired ...

A beam of light stabbed through Simon's pupils. He tried to cry out, but his voice had deserted him when he first fell ill.

"Nope." Loud. Far too loud. He wanted to cover his ears but only managed to roll his head to one side.

"No good for questioning anymore?"

The light shone again, firing pain to the back of Simon's brain.

"You could always try, but I doubt you'll get anywhere."

"Well, I'll see what the lieutenant says. Probably let him go."

"Do you want to take him to the infirmary?"

Simon tried to breathe, but it took several failed attempts before his lungs filled up with even the smallest trace of air.

"Sounds like more trouble than it's worth. I suppose we could call in the nurse, though. Have her take a look."

"Nurse or not, can't be more than a day or two, don't you think?"

Simon's tongue rolled back over his airway. He forced his head to the side and managed to inhale.

"Days, hours, same difference."

Silence fell. No more blinding light. Funny how the darkness didn't bother him the way it used to. To sleep, to never have to struggle again.

Simon shut his eyes.

***

"Here's the patient I told you about."

"How long has he been sick?" The voices carried through the fog of Simon's dreamless sleep.

"Don't remember. He's in bad shape. Doubt you'll do him much good."

"Then I'll try to make him as comfortable as possible."

Bars rattled. Gentle steps, soft as the spring breeze, tiptoed toward him. A hallucination, but such a beautiful one. He pried his eyes open. An angel? She sat and cradled his head in her lap. He tried to lift his chin, but it was too heavy.

"I'm sorry to hear you've been sick." The voice was radiant as a ray of heavenly glory, but something about it still tied him to this earth. He swallowed once. He had to focus.

She adjusted her flashlight, and in that split second, everything was clear. She gasped, and then a look of horror chased away the shock on her face. She clutched his frail shoulders. Fear rushed through his veins, diluted by a flood of joy that threatened to sweep him away in a delightful, terrifying torrent. He tried to speak but couldn't. For a moment, he realized he must be dead until he heard the gasping rattle from his own lungs.

She whispered his name. Once. Twice. He prayed with a fervency he had never known, focusing all his spiritual energy into one single word: *Please*. She leaned down over him, and her warm tears splashed onto his face, reviving him, awakening his spirit that had been so ready to rest, reminding him just how badly he wanted to live.

Oh, sweet and merciful Jesus, he wanted to live.

CHAPTER 25

Hannah. She had come to him, tended to him. It was more real than any of his previous visions. He groaned when he woke, unwilling for the dream to end.

"Do you hurt much?" The voice was pristine, beautiful. The surge of energy that shot through him forced out a violent cough.

He blinked. "Not dreaming?" The laughter that rang out was sweeter than cool water from the freshest mountain stream. He reached his hand up to stroke her cheek and felt strong enough to dance. "Where are we?"

"The infirmary. I told them I'd help you recover. Said you might even work again in the mines." Her fingers traced the veins on his forearm.

He opened his mouth and tried several times to speak. "I thought I'd never see you again."

"Shhh." She glanced over her shoulder and then picked up a small tube. She dipped her finger into something creamy, leaned over, and with a touch that made his chest nearly explode from fullness, she spread the lotion across his chapped lips.

He still didn't understand. This certainly wasn't heaven. How had he been delivered from his deathbed in a cold, dark cell and transferred to this room with light, with warmth, with her? It was more than his mind could take in all at once.

She placed a damp rag on his forehead. "The fever's already breaking." She swept a clump of his sweaty hair off his brow. "You're going to live."

***

Hannah didn't sleep until the following morning, when Simon's breathing eased enough she could spare a short nap. She woke up in the chair by his bed. The sun shone bright through the infirmary window, warming her shoulders and cheeks. She stood up clumsily, her joints stiff, but when she saw Simon smiling, all her aches vanished. She felt his forehead, letting her hand linger on his face even after she convinced herself he was still improving. "You look better."

"You look beautiful."

Her fingers still stroked his cheek.

"Nurse?" a voice rasped behind them. "Nurse." Hannah lingered near Simon's side for just a moment longer before squeezing his hand and turning to the next bed. By the time she helped her patient drink a little bit of water, two other prisoners across the room were calling for her. She felt Simon's eyes on her the entire time she tended them, and her pulse didn't slow down until she returned to his side.

"You're an angel." Simon was pale, but not ghastly gray like last night when she convinced the guards to bring him to the infirmary.

Simon wiggled his finger. He had lost a lot of weight since they left Yanji. He looked so weak lying on the blood-stained gurney. But they were together again. Nothing else mattered. She rested her head on his pillow. He whispered something, but she couldn't make it out.

"Nurse?" The cry sounded from several beds over.

"I can't stay." She yearned to nuzzle her face into that soft spot between his chin and shoulder, to rest in the comfort of his presence, to forget about prison camps and infirmaries and dying inmates. But she resisted the gravity that tugged her entire being toward him, and she forced herself to stand. "I'll come back soon."

***

Simon's strength flourished each day he spent under Hannah's tender watch. The infirmary food wasn't any more wholesome than what they fed him in solitary, but the portions were larger, and Hannah made sure he ate everything they served. If he wasn't careful, she would even sneak some of her own rations into his bowl.

As his fever cleared, his mind regained some of the clarity he lost in the darkness downstairs. He wanted to know what had happened to Hannah, but they could never talk privately. She had dozens of patients to care for, and the officers kept constant guard over them all. And so Simon observed the way she moved from one bed to another with a grace and dignity that had only matured since she left the Secret Seminary. In spite of the infirmary's squalid conditions, her whole being radiated peace. She moved slowly, weighed down by invisible burdens, but she cared for the sick and the dying with a tenderness that left him speechless. Men reached out to her, called for her all hours of the night. Women held onto her hand as they breathed their last, and she closed their eyelids with gentle fingers.

Without realizing it, Simon began to daydream about the future, a future outside the infirmary, outside Camp 22's electric fence. He remembered his comrades' discussions about Moses. What if he wasn't a myth? What if there really was such a man, a champion for Christian prisoners? Would he help Hannah and Simon escape? If they could just get to Yanji, the Sterns could arrange for them to immigrate to South Korea or the United States. They could get married, start a family …

Hannah ran a rag over his forehead, interrupting his impossible daydream. "What are you thinking about?"

Simon stroked her forearm, his callouses drinking up the silky smoothness of her skin. "I was just picturing what a beautiful mother you'd make." She turned away for a moment, but not before her cheeks betrayed a faint blush. He tilted her face toward him. "I love you," he whispered. "You know that, don't you?" He stroked her chin with his dry, cracked thumb.

"I know," she replied. Her downcast eyes couldn't hide her radiance. Her lips looked so soft, so kissable. "I've always known."

CHAPTER 26

She could hardly lift her feet as she shuffled down the corridor. Simon was strong enough to walk on his own now, but she wrapped her arm around his waist anyway. She could feel his whole body sigh, and she sensed the heaviness loaded in that one single breath. Her throat constricted. She bit the inside of her cheek.

Six days. After Chongjin jailors tore him away, after they survived months of separation, the Lord gave her a mere six days. Six days tending to his wounds, soothing his scars, loving him with the healing touch that flowed so readily from her fingertips.

And now it was over. At least with Simon in the general prison cells, she could check on him every few days. But then what? When the National Security agents decided he was strong enough, what would stop them from sending him back to the mines? How could his body survive such abuse? How could her spirit endure losing him again?

Her legs grew heavier with each step. She tried to focus on the verses she learned at the Secret Seminary, but today they were nothing more than empty words. There were no platitudes, no proverbs, no promises to comfort her now. Sometimes she wondered why God reunited them in the first place. Why torment them with a single glimpse of bliss? Even allowing them to die together would have been more merciful.

She didn't realize how slow their pace had fallen until they both stopped at the same spot. A light buzzed around the corner, the last turn before they reached the cells. She longed to dissolve with him into the shadows forever. "I don't want to go," she confessed.

He bent his face down to hers. The lights flickered off, leaving only a high-pitched hum. "I know." He wrapped his arms around her, drawing her toward his chest.

She took a deep breath, trying to inhale his strength, his nearness. His lips grazed her cheek, and she pulled herself deeper into the shadows, deeper into him. The salty taste of tears lingered on the corner of her mouth. She lifted her chin, knowing his lips would be there waiting. She tried to gasp when he reached down, but it only deepened their kiss.

She was breathless when he lifted his face and cupped her cheeks in his hands. "I'm sorry," he whispered. "I shouldn't have …"

She closed her eyes and wrapped both arms around his neck, the fire in her belly urging her closer as she kissed him again. When he pulled away, both their faces were wet from tears. She rested her cheek on his shoulder. The coarse fabric of his prison garment scratched her skin. The light buzzed on once more. She pressed her hand against her temple, which was throbbing in sync with his heart. He took a choppy breath and let it out slowly. Her stomach fell, and she realized it was time.

"I love you," she breathed. They didn't look at each other. His lips gently brushed the top of her head. He squeezed her hand once, and she pried herself away from him. She forbid her tears from falling as she watched him walk ahead, and she wondered how such glorious love could flourish alongside such despair.

***

Anything had to be better than solitary confinement.

Simon studied his new cellmates. Some gave him nothing more than a fleeting glance, while a few glared with open suspicion. Others remained frozen in place, statues with only the slightest indication of life.

His lips burned where they had touched hers. He shut his eyes, his gut replaying the dropping sensation he experienced when she kissed him back. The cell reeked, a mixture of human waste and rampant infection, but somewhere in the back of his mind flitted the scent of Mrs. Stern's roses. As the barred door locked behind him, he kept his eyes warily on the other prisoners.

"Brother Simon?" The voice was hoarse, gravelly. The speaker was short, but his skinniness couldn't mask his wide, sturdy build. His white hair flopped down in a tangled mess over his brow.

"Mal-Chin?" The name caught in Simon's throat. He strained to see the back of his old friend's head where the National Security agent had bashed it in during the raid. "How are you?"

Mal-Chin offered a smile that looked to Simon more like a grimace. "I'm alive."

"I saw you injured that night. I thought you … I thought we lost you."

Mal-Chin closed his eyes for a moment. "I had hoped, Brother. I admit, I had hoped."

"But you recovered?"

"I recovered. They kept me in underground for a while." Mal-Chin kept his voice low. "Turns out I didn't know what they wanted me to know."

"I was down there, too. Just got out a few days ago." Simon stretched his legs out, a luxury he had never experienced in his solitary cell. "I got sick, so they brought me to the infirmary."

"I was there once too. A nurse — pretty little prisoner — she helped me heal up." Simon stared at his hands and said nothing. Mal-Chin's voice grew distant. "Tiny wisp of a thing. Tender as an angel."

Simon swallowed. "How do they treat you here?"

Mal-Chin shrugged. "Can't complain. Rations are about half

what they fed us in the mines, but we sometimes find a rat. Beatings only once or twice a week. I feel like I'm on holiday." His chuckle quickly morphed into a cough.

Simon didn't know what else to say. He wanted to tell Mal-Chin about Hannah, but he couldn't. Not here. The National Security Agency could never learn about their relationship. It was the one thing he could do to keep her safe. He would keep his memories in the most sacred storehouses of his mind, pretending to forget the warmth of her touch, the surge of power that swept over him just a few minutes earlier. His stomach still felt like he was falling.

"I'm glad you're all right," Simon finally admitted. Mal-Chin didn't respond. "I'm glad we're together."

***

Hannah's lips tingled. An electric zing raced up her spine. If she focused hard enough, she could still detect his smell lingering on her clothes. She knew soon the scent would vanish, and she would lose hours of sleep trying to recapture its essence.

Her heart raced, but her body moved as if against a flowing river. Simon was alive, he was out of solitary confinement. The Lord had spared his life — had spared both of their lives — but for what purpose? So they could spend the rest of their time on earth separated by iron bars? When she left the Secret Seminary, she had been ready for anything. She was willing to accept a life without Simon, a life full of danger and sacrifice. She was even prepared to die for the gospel. And then Simon came back, reigniting an impossible, forbidden passion in her heart. And why? Just so he could be ripped away from her once more? Was God punishing her for loving him too much? She had already given up her safety and expectations for any sort of future. Did God expect her to give up Simon just as easily, especially after what they had just shared together?

Things could have been so different. She thought about the day Simon found her in Mrs. Stern's garden and told her his news. Mr. Stern knew of a Korean-speaking church in the United States that needed a pastor. He thought Simon would be an ideal candidate for the position.

"Are you really thinking of going?" she had asked, amazed he could even fathom serving the Lord anywhere but North Korea.

Simon's answer had been cryptic. "I wanted to ask your opinion before I made any decisions."

And like the fool she was, she told him to do whatever God called him to do and promised to pray for him no matter what. Even then, she had noted the disappointment in his eyes, as if he had expected something much more from her. If only they had known what trials awaited them across the border. If only they hadn't ignored their feelings and concealed the truth even from themselves.

A church in the United States. A congregation to shepherd. Maybe even a family to raise in time. If he had asked her to go with him way back then, would she have said yes? Yes to a life in America, with its fast-food restaurants and skyscrapers? If he told her that he wanted to marry her, would she have followed him? Could she have torn herself away from her dream of returning to her people, her homeland?

It didn't matter. She sniffed. Regrets were as big a waste as her tears. Hannah bit her lip. She had to seize control of her thoughts. There was no way to change anything. At least now she could visit Simon in the general cells and make sure he was all right. Wasn't that what she had always wanted — to know he was safe? God had given her that ... and so much more. Her repose with Simon was a blessing she wouldn't have dared hope for. And now that it was over, she would just have to go on with her duties in the infirmary. She had been at Camp 22 long enough to know life could be horrifically worse.

She would be thankful. She would pray for Simon, treasure his memory, dream about his kiss every single night and every waking moment. And she would remember he was a blessing — a blessing she hadn't asked for and never did anything to deserve. She swept her eyes over the rows of beds, the patients who would need her care tonight. She had a meaningful calling here, which was more than most prisoners at Camp 22 could say. She swallowed away the lump in her throat, licked her lip, and lifted her chin.

There was work to do.

First, she went to the old man they brought in last night. She hadn't had a chance to share the gospel with him yet, but she knew from the death rattle in his lungs and the ashen color of his skin that his time was running out. She checked his erratic pulse and begged God to wait just a little longer. Had she spent so much energy taking care of Simon she had neglected those patients who needed her even more? Was that the reason God took him away? Was he just a distraction from her real ministry here in the infirmary?

Hannah leaned down and trickled water from a dropper into the old man's mouth. It dribbled down his chin. She bit her cheek and wondered if God was angry with her. She glanced over her shoulder. There were two guards in the infirmary. If only they would leave ... *Please*, she prayed, *I only need a few minutes.*

One of the guards tossed a clipboard onto a metal tray and strode out. Hope rose in Hannah's spirit. Maybe God wasn't disgusted with her after all. Maybe he was giving her another chance to witness to this dying man. She glanced around.

"Am I interrupting something?"

Hannah's head jerked up at the sound of the nasally whine. She turned to face the large nose of the infirmary's assistant director and tried to will away her flush. "I was just ..."

He snorted. "I know what you were doing. I also know who you were with just a few minutes ago."

His leering eyes bored into her. He grabbed her arm and tugged her away from her patient and toward a dark hallway. "Don't worry." His mouth curled up in a snarl that chilled her marrow. "I'll make sure your boyfriend doesn't know about our time together. These halls aren't as dark as you'd like to think."

The assistant director's nose had a prominent curve at the tip, like the beak of a vulture. Hannah bit her lip to keep it from quivering. She could still see some of the patients' beds. Surely he wouldn't hurt her here.

"The Chief Officer of Productivity would be very displeased if he knew about you and your ... friend."

He flung her to the ground. Hannah shut her eyes. All she wanted was to return to the infirmary. God wouldn't allow him to harm her, would he?

"There's one way you could make me forget what I saw and keep your boyfriend out of trouble. Want to guess what it is?" He squatted down beside her and fingered her chin. "Don't worry." His breath burned hot like acid on her shoulder. "You'll like it as much as I will."

Her whole body tensed, and she imagined an iron cocoon enveloping her, protecting her. Sweat from his stubbly cheeks smeared across her face, and in a moment, his lips were against hers, hard, angry, fierce. Stifling her scream, she tried to push him away, but he dug his fingers into the flesh of her arms. She swallowed down bile. After the kiss, he ran his sleeve across his mouth and stood up. She rolled herself into a ball and covered her face.

"I told you that you'd like it," he sneered over his shoulder and strode away.

She let out her breath slowly, like the controlled, measured hiss of Mrs. Stern's tea kettle. She needed a drink, a shower, some way to wash off his filth. A hollow gnawing in the pit of her stomach bent her over when she tried to stand. She kept one hand on the wall as she stumbled along. Back in the infirmary, she swept her gaze over the patients who had no idea what just happened. Her last bit of strength failed her when she saw two prison orderlies bending over the old man. His body was wrapped up in a sheet, and they hefted both ends on their shoulders, letting the corpse sway back and forth between them. She felt her legs start to buckle, and she reached out to lean against the wall.

It was too late.

CHAPTER 27

Hannah kept her steps slow, but her pulse raced as she walked down the hall toward Simon's cell. She had managed to avoid the assistant director for several days, but whenever she passed his office, the skin on the back of her neck still tingled. She stayed as busy as always, but her energy was gone. What difference did any of her work make? Nearly all the patients she cared for died anyway. A weariness hung over her, a heavy mist no amount of prayers or good deeds could lift.

Even the prospect of visiting Simon again left her heavy and cold as she rounded the last corner of the hallway. Before the cells came into view, she heard the sound of prisoners, their bodies shuffling, their bare feet pacing, dozens of men breathing, breathing in spite of the squalor, in spite of the starvation, in spite of the disease that infested the ward.

She pressed her lips together. In the past week, Hannah had grown to loathe Camp 22 with an icy hatred totally foreign to her. This was all that came from her grand plans, her lofty aspirations. Here she was, alone, afraid, ashamed of sins that hadn't even been committed against her. When she first started studying Psalms at the Secret Seminary, she had snubbed David for feeling rejected. Now she knew Christians really could be abandoned in the valley of the shadow of death. Victory wasn't guaranteed. She thought back to her training when she was certain she would sense God's presence no matter what befell her. She would look upon her persecutors and love them with the passion of Christ. She would tend to the hopeless with a faith that overcame all darkness and fear. She was ashamed of her former self, ashamed of the blind optimism, the overwhelming pride, the assumption she could withstand all manner of evil.

As she passed cell after cell of prisoners, Hannah recognized in their eyes the same resignation that hung heavy over her own soul. Every inmate at Camp 22 was her brother or sister in suffering, but she was entirely alone.

***

His head was throbbing, but he sensed her approach before he saw her, sensed it in the collective inhale of the inmates around him, in their tense bodies and curious gazes. He couldn't run to her. Her eyes flitted up to his, and he felt the same jolt of electricity pass through him that he experienced every time he remembered the sweet taste of her lips. She said something to the guard. Simon wiped beads of sweat off his brow.

"She the one took care of you?" Mal-Chin asked.

On the opposite side of the bars, Hannah pointed at Simon. The guard frowned but beckoned him over, unlocking the cell door lazily. "Nurse's here to give you a looking over."

Simon felt the hard stares of his cellmates. When Hannah stepped in, waves of protective jealousy swirled around in his belly. Her chin trembled slightly when she walked up to him. "How do you feel?"

His eyes drank her in. He missed nothing in her face, the worry lines pulling her lips downward, the heavy wrinkles across her brow. He imagined reaching out, sweeping her hair behind her ear, stroking her cheek as he had dreamed so often these past few days. His arms hung limp and useless at his sides. "I'm all right. How are you?"

"I came to check on you." Her voice was quiet, detached, but her lower lip quivered.

"I'm feeling better. I've been worried," he added.

"I know." Her eyes darted to the side, and Simon wondered what price he'd be willing to pay in exchange for a quiet room to talk with her in private. Would the rest of their relationship be like this — clinical, sterile, censored?

He sighed. "It's good to see you."

She reached up toward him, and his heart quickened even though he knew there would be no embrace. She laid her hand on his forehead, her expression unreadable. "You don't feel feverish."

There was nothing to say, but everything remained unspoken. He saw she was already about to leave, noted the sad, determined look in her eyes, and he reached out his hand, stopping just short of touching her. "It was ..." His throat constricted. The glowers of his cellmates burned his skin. "It was good of you to check on me."

She nodded once, and he read in that single gesture the same emptiness that had burrowed its way into his own heart. The guard let her out, and Simon turned away, not even trusting himself to watch her depart. He crouched on the floor, where Mal-Chin joined him. Minutes dragged by in silence.

"She's a friend of mine." Simon stared straight ahead. He wasn't even sure the old man heard.

"You meet in the infirmary?" Mal-Chin finally asked.

Simon scratched his forehead.

"She took care of me there, too." Mal-Chin smudged some dirt on his uniform. "Nice girl."

The electricity buzzed off, and the old man eventually drifted to sleep. Simon stayed awake, wondering how many more times he would see Hannah before death freed them from this incessant torment.

CHAPTER 28

"It's you." The prisoner beside her reached up a shaking hand. Hannah clasped it warmly. With her free arm, she adjusted the blanket around his shoulders. Someone cleared his throat behind her.

She recognized the assistant director's voice instantly and willed her hands not to tremble. She bent down over the patient. "I'll be back to check on you soon." She didn't know if it was a lie or not. For a second, she thought about hurrying to another bedside, but retreat was pointless. He grabbed her wrist before she even turned around. Her entire being cringed inward, as if she could collapse inside herself and disappear.

"I hear you made a little visit today."

"Yes, sir." Fear wrapped its tendrils around Hannah's throat.

He chuckled mirthlessly. "See anybody special while you were there?" He drew his words out slowly.

"I was just checking on a patient." She tidied up a stash of medical supplies and tried to step toward the next bed.

"I'm not done talking to you." He whipped her around, digging his fingernails into her arm. "You need to learn a little respect." He dragged her past rows of beds, forcing her to run at times to keep up.

Clumps of hair flopped down her forehead, but she didn't sweep them out of her eyes. *He's not going to let you go this time, you know.* Sweat dripped down from her armpits by the time he threw her into the office and slammed the door shut behind them. Everything was chaotic and choppy, like one of Mrs. Stern's movies when the disc got dirty. Screaming was pointless. The prisoners who could hear her were powerless to respond, and the guards nearby had no reason to intervene.

She leapt away as the assistant director lumbered toward her. "Get over here."

She tried to lunge past him, but he punched her hard across the cheek. Her head snapped back, and she lost her balance. She fell and thrashed her arms behind her, searching for some way to ward him off. Her fingers grasped a meter stick. She slashed it through the air but couldn't even see clearly to aim.

He growled and flung the useless weapon out of her hands. She crouched down into a ball, trying to cover as much of herself as she could. He yanked her up by the hair, and then he slammed her against the wall. Vice-like fingers pinched her neck.

His thumb pressed against her throat, just enough to keep her from squealing. "That's enough." He squeezed a little harder until she let out a tiny nod. "No more fighting. Got that?"

She bit the inside of her cheek, certain she wouldn't be able to keep down the great swells of nausea crashing around inside her. Her heart beat against her chest like a trapped bird, frantic for freedom, and she shut her eyes. This wasn't happening. It wasn't real. After everything she had already endured, God wouldn't allow this. It was a nightmare and nothing more, a nightmare she would tell Simon about when they woke up in the morning at the Sterns' house. He would comfort her, assure her it was only a bad dream. Simon loved her. He would never let anybody hurt her.

"Look at me." The pressure of the assistant director's thumb on her throat induced a gag, and her eyelids flung open. His lip curled upward. "That's better." He leaned even closer, and she had to swallow down the first rush of vomit. He shoved her against the desk, and she threw her hands behind her to catch her fall. He was against her in an instant, sneering, pressing with every part of his sharp, knobby body. "Did your boyfriend have anything to say to you? Did you give him a kiss good-bye?" His breath reeked of rot and onions.

She shut her eyes and gritted her teeth. How would she face Simon after this? She put her hands up to push the assistant director away, but he gripped both her wrists and wrenched her hands back again. She kicked her legs wildly. If she could only get her feet back on the floor ... She tossed her head back and forth, desperate for enough momentum to throw him off.

"It's no use." Tiny drops of his spit sprayed onto her cheeks. "I saw the way you acted. I know you want this as much as I do."

Without any plan, she thrust out her arm and clenched a handful of his hair. He roared and clawed at her cheek, trying to gouge her eye. A second later, his hand encircled her throat. She clawed to free herself. White specks floated in her field of vision. She had already lost the battle.

He tightened his grip for a moment and shook her. "I said no more fighting." He spoke the words with an icy calm that chilled her all the way down to the inside of her bones.

She strained for air, certain she could endure whatever humiliation was to come as long as he let her breathe again.

The door latch rattled in its lock, and someone pounded outside. The assistant director swore and released his hold. She collapsed and dropped to the floor, coughing until her ribs ached. When he stepped away, she scrambled under the desk and shivered while he conversed with her unsuspecting savior. Once the meeting ended, the assistant director stormed out, slamming the door behind him. She remained hidden, expecting his boots to materialize in front of her at any moment. It was a long time before she realized she was free, and still longer before she found enough courage and strength to creep back to the infirmary.

How had she ever felt at home in Camp 22? How had she ever felt safe walking its dark hallways? She licked her bottom lip and tucked her hair behind her ears. She wouldn't think about the assistant director and his hooked nose. She wouldn't think about what he had almost done to her in his back office. Her body still quivered, but she had work to do. Important work. Work that no degree of terror could snatch away from her.

She sucked in her lower lip. Her whole face stung, and she wondered if the assistant director had smashed in some of her bones. It didn't matter. There were people here who needed her. Earlier the guards brought in a teenager with multiple wounds from her interrogations. The humiliation Hannah suffered tonight was nothing in comparison. She should just be grateful for whoever was at the door. It could have gotten much worse.

She went to the teenager's bedside, her legs still shaky. Something about the girl tugged on Hannah's spirit, and she felt certain the child was covered by the Holy Spirit. Hannah could almost feel the intercession like a protective shield and knew someone had prayed for her. She stopped long enough to glance around at the patients in the infirmary. Had any of the other inmates been bathed in prayer like this? As she applied an antibacterial salve to some infected cuts, she wondered if it really mattered in the end. The girl's wounds were quite extensive. The National Security Agency hadn't held back on account of her youth.

"Is the pain very bad?" Hannah asked.

The girl didn't respond but stared at the ceiling with a glazed expression. Sometimes Hannah dreamed of putting herself into such a psychological cocoon until her body gave out and released her soul to heaven. "It's going to get better." She tucked one hand behind the girl's head and slowly propped her up to drink a little water. "I don't know if you're able to believe me right now, but I want you to know it's true." Conviction swelled and infused her words. *"Weeping may endure for a night, but joy comes in the morning."* Hannah felt the words minister to her own soul. She stayed by the girl's side for a full hour, breathing

Scripture that filled her aching spirit and soothed over so many wounds.

***

Officer Lang glowered out his office window. The infirmary nurse leaned over a haggard, skeletal girl. She stroked the patient's hair and wore an imbecilic, benign look on her face. He clenched his teeth until his jaw muscle throbbed in time with his pulse. He had almost had her. Nervous excitement raced up and down his legs as he thought about how close he had come. If only Officer Yeong hadn't intruded. But Yeong was one of Camp 22's powerful elite. If Lang wanted to advance anywhere in his career, he had to kowtow to idiots like that, even if it lost him his evening's amusement.

He scratched the hollow of his cheek with the back of a pen. She was weak. He could go over now and take her, but the interruption had spoiled his appetite. *"More order,"* Yeong had demanded. The newly-appointed Chief Officer of Productivity was just itching to show the leaders in Pyongyang the full prowess of the Camp 22 labor machine. Higher quotas, longer hours, more structure, even for the prisoners in the detainment center. *"Demonstrate our authority,"* Yeong had admonished. *"These types only respond to fear."* Yeong droned on for so long it drained Lang of all desire and only left him irritable. Now he was stuck working impossibly late hours without even the chance of a diversion.

He stared at her in disgust. Who did she think she was, parading around the infirmary like some angel on a pathetic mission of mercy? The beasts on those cots didn't deserve her compassion. They were slaves. Slaves, traitors, and criminals. Why should she waste her sweet words and loving touches on scum like them? Lang had flipped through her file several times. Arrested for selling state secrets, consorting with known national traitors. He saw through their lies. She was no spy. She had probably been caught at the border and refused to give the lusty guard whatever bribe he demanded, so he trumped up the charges to get back at her.

Lang scratched his scalp and thought about how she had fought him off. She didn't realize what kind of power she was toying with. She preferred to keep company with prisoners, then. He would show her what kind of mistake she had made. One corner of his lip curled into a half-snarl. He would get back at her. And when he was done, she'd be begging him to take her, dying for the chance to make things right.

But by then, it would be too late.

CHAPTER 29

The first thing Simon noticed when she came to him that morning was her neck. As soon as the guard let her in the cell, Simon rushed up. "What happened?" With little regard for potential onlookers, he fingered the blaring streaks of blue and purple.

Her throat quivered. "I just came to see how you're feeling."

"Who did this to you?"

When she finally looked up at him, her eyes gleamed with such unspeakable sorrow, he hardly even recognized her. She felt his forehead and cheeks. "No fever. You haven't been sweating much?"

He balled his hands into fists. "Who hurt you?"

"How has your appetite been?"

He hated this charade, this game. He envisioned taking her into his arms and holding her until the National Security agents came and tore them apart. He was willing to die for one last embrace, but he wouldn't jeopardize her safety. "I'm hungry," he admitted in defeat.

She nodded without smiling. "Your digestion must be improving."

He ran one hand through her hair and studied her injuries. Dark bruises radiated outward, highlighted by purple splotches on the side of her throat. Her eye was dark and swollen. "Any other complications?" she asked him. "Chills? Pain?"

He didn't know if he wanted to shake her or kiss her. "I'm fine."

She bit her lip. "Good." They tarried for a moment, and Simon remembered the warmth of her lips on his, the weight of her body pressed against his chest. "I'll see you soon." There was no emotion in her voice or in her expression. She nodded once to the guard and left the cell. Simon leaned against the wall and let his heavy body sink to the floor, wondering if he would ever hold her again. He thought about their time together in Yanji, the conversations they shared in Mrs. Stern's flower garden. He was a fool for not telling her then how much he loved her. He was a fool for letting her cross the border alone. Could he ever forgive himself for all the mistakes he had made, all the pain he had caused her?

Half an hour or so after she left, a shrill whistle forced Simon and the rest of his cellmates to their feet. The assistant director flew by, barking orders. "Up, all of you. At attention. Now." Lang accentuated each command with a piercing screech from his whistle.

"He's at it early," Simon mumbled.

"Must be an inspection day," Mal-Chin remarked.

The men formed their lines and waited to count off. It was strange having the assistant director there. Usually shift guards oversaw roll-call, and then only when they happened to remember it. Simon couldn't be certain, but he thought Lang glared directly at him. Simon swallowed once and straightened his back as much as he could.

The assistant director stopped and pointed his beaked nose right at Simon. "You. 39846." He raised a finger, as if anyone could doubt whom he addressed. "Follow me."

Simon didn't return Mal-Chin's gaze. If Simon was in trouble, he had to keep his friend out of it. As he followed the assistant director out the cell, he racked his brain, trying to think of any of the camp rules he might have broken. Was Hannah in trouble for visiting him? Did this have something to do with her? Why did they ever leave Yanji?

Once in his office, Lang made a slow show of scooting back his chair and lowering himself into it with a flourish. Simon remained standing and gazed at the metal desk between them.

"I've been watching you." Lang scratched his gigantic nose. Simon tried to keep his face neutral. "Shift guards say you're no trouble."

"Yes, sir." Simon wondered when the compliment would reveal its poisonous barb.

"A strong young man like you isn't meant for life behind bars. You want to be out working, don't you? Serving your nation."

Simon shifted his feet. "Yes, sir." Were they sending him back to the mines? He swallowed down his anxiety. Would he ever see her again?

The assistant director nodded, keeping his bug-eyed pupils fixed on Simon. "Good. I have an assignment for you."

Simon waited, uncertain if this revelation warranted another *Yes, sir* or not.

"I got a pen and paper here. And you, you're going to write down all the prisoners who complain. Nothing fancy. You just write me their names and what they're whining about and pass it to the guards." The assistant director raised an eyebrow. "That a problem, prisoner?" His voice dripped with concern, but hostility gleamed from his stare.

Simon straightened his back. His face throbbed where the shovel had smashed him months earlier. "No, sir."

Lang slid his chair noisily back and circled him with slow, deliberate strides. "I've just given you one of the highest honors a prisoner in your position could hope for."

Simon's throat felt as dry as the parched countryside during the worst of the Great Famine. "Thank you, Officer."

Lang harrumphed and took a step closer. "You're still not happy." He leaned in, and Simon was certain he saw a spark of malicious delight shimmer in Lang's eye.

"I appreciate the honor, sir, and will carry out my duties as best I can."

"Good." Lang handed Simon a small cloth bag with long drawstrings. "Tie this around your waist. Guard on duty will collect your notes each morning." Simon wondered why Lang even bothered to give him a secret bag. Prisoners could sniff out a traitor even more skillfully than they hunted rats. This "honor" was a death sentence of its own kind. Lang opened the office door and beckoned a guard. "Take him back to his cell."

Simon's legs were heavy as he turned to go.

"Wait. One more thing." There was a hint of pleasure in Lang's voice. "We can't have your cellmates getting suspicious." Lang gave a nod, and the guard at the door took a step closer. "You go back there unharmed, and they'll know exactly what we talked about."

Simon had just enough time to suck in his breath before the attack began.

***

Lang wiped his shoe with a rag and smiled smugly as 39846 limped out of his office. The National Security Agency had discovered long ago there was no simpler way to turn cellmates against one another than to send a mole into their ranks. With Officer Yeong breathing down his neck about productivity and morale, Lang could rest assured that 39846 was serving multiple purposes. The prisoners would be on better behavior, at least until they smelled out the traitor. And when they discovered who it was, the nurse's boyfriend would bear the brunt of their anger. That should make her regret flitting away from him last night. Maybe once his cellmates were good and done with him, Lang would send 39846 back to the infirmary and let his little girlfriend try to sew him back together. What did the flirt see in him besides a bony figure in clothes twice too big? Lang shrugged and picked up his pen. She could have had a real man.

Now, she would only have a corpse.

***

Simon's eye was so swollen he could scarcely see. Blood dripped from his mouth, and he guessed from the way his head wanted to tilt lopsided that his nose was broken. He coughed weakly, his ribs screeching in pain from the effort. The other prisoners took a few collective steps back as the guard opened the gate and dumped Simon onto the floor.

"What was that for?" There was no shock or anger in Mal-Chin's voice, only a tender, tired sort of concern.

Simon tried to shrug and ended up groaning instead. He heard the sound of ripping cloth. "Here." A young man with two fingers missing held out a strip of uniform-gray cloth from his uniform. "Use it to stop the bleeding."

Simon groaned again as Mal-Chin wadded up the rag and shoved it against his nose. He needed to cough, but his body wouldn't respond.

"You'll be all right." Mal-Chin spoke with a certain air of authority. "We're all going to be all right."

Several others came closer. Their voices floated in and out of Simon's consciousness. His head ached. Sharp, icy splinters jabbed into his chest with each breath. Mal-Chin cradled his head and crooned meaningless pleasantries into his ear in a soothing, melodic tone. Someone held the cloth to his bleeding nose, while another prodded his legs and torso.

"I don't think anything's broken."

"Bleeding's slowing down." Simon recognized the voice of the boy with the missing fingers.

"Wonder what the assistant director wanted with him."

"Doesn't matter," someone else answered. "Don't need a reason if you're National Security."

A few men murmured their agreements. Simon wanted to warn them. Didn't they know how dangerous it was to talk that way? Didn't they know he'd have to report everything he heard?

"How's he doing?" another cellmate asked.

"All right," Mal-Chin answered. "Just roughed up a little."

"Nothing serious?"

"No. He'll be back on his feet by the end of the day. A little sore, I'd wager, but he'll be all right."

Simon wanted to tell the others to stop worrying about him. They wouldn't be so caring if they knew of his assignment from Lang. And once they found him out, he'd be even worse off than now. Maybe that's what the assistant director had in mind from the beginning. Simon's head felt as though it was cloven in two, with pain radiating out into both hemispheres symmetrically.

"Try to get some rest now." Mal-Chin tossed the drenched rag in the corner, and Simon was too exhausted to do anything but comply.

***

"Excuse me, sir."

Lang turned away from the window overlooking the infirmary. He glared at the secretary who interrupted his vigil. "What do you want?"

"The Chief Officer of Productivity is here to see you." The secretary bowed once and scurried backward out of the office. Officer Yeong came in a second later, his spine rigid, his face set.

Lang snapped to attention. "Good morning, Comrade Officer."

Yeong grunted in response and sat down in Lang's chair. "What headway has been made regarding prisoner morale?"

Lang glared at his seat, but he willed himself to smile. "Plenty. I got one of the inmates to keep me informed. I expect that in a week or less, we'll have an end to all the complaints. I'm also in the process of developing a more regimented schedule so the men don't get used to idleness."

Yeong crossed his arms. "Is that all?" His tone was incredulous.

"I've only had a few hours since our discussion last night. Surely you don't expect ..."

"What I expect," Yeong snapped, "is compliance. Your new procedures will be approved and implemented before the Day of the Sun. Am I clear?"

"Yes. Perfectly."

The Chief Officer of Productivity stood and swept out the office without a parting bow. Lang watched him leave. He'd have killed for a cigarette. He picked up the phone and radioed his secretary.

"Get in here."

The underling hurried in just seconds later, fidgeting with his fingers. "What is it, sir?"

"We got work to discuss." Lang scratched his chin and scowled. "I've got Yeong breathing down my neck at every step. Says he wants more order. More control. More productivity." Lang spat out the last word and threw up his hands. What did Yeong expect? This was a prison ward, not a factory. The men were hardened, idle criminals, good for interrogating and spying on each other and nothing else. Productivity? How could you even measure that here?

The secretary kept his eyes on Lang's desk. "We can augment the schedule we drafted last night."

Lang flung down his pen. It wasn't a cigarette, but until he found favor with one of his superiors and caught them in a generous mood, he'd be stuck waving writing utensils around like an imbecile. "We're not going to impress Yeong by scribbling nonsense on calendars."

The secretary at least knew enough to keep his mouth shut. Lang paced back and forth by the window, staring out at the infirmary. Where was that little nurse? If Yeong hadn't started acting like such a feudal tyrant lord last night, Lang might still have some of his appetite left. Oh, well. He had other plans for her now anyway.

"What do you have in mind?" The secretary poised his pencil above his notebook. Lang ignored the urge to hurl a chair at him. The kid was an idiot without a single creative thought to his credit. What Lang needed was something huge. Something unforgettable. Something he could stamp his name all over and shove under the noses of all those Pyongyang aristocrats. What he needed was big. Grand.

"A demonstration." The word erupted from Lang's mouth before his brain finished registering the idea.

"Sir?" The secretary stood there, looking stupid and confused as always, but at least he was respectful. He knew what it was to fear his superiors.

Lang grabbed another pen from his desk and jabbed at an imaginary speck in the air. "A demonstration." The faster he spoke, the more the idea appealed to him. "We find the worst offenders here. Shouldn't be tricky. And we make examples of them for everyone else, including our new Chief Officer." He glanced at the calendar on his desk. "How long before the Day of the Sun?"

"Two days, sir." At least the fool knew how to count.

Lang pressed his forehead against the window. "Then we have work to do." A smirk tugged at the corner of his lip when he spotted the little nurse spoon-feeding the victim of a mining accident. Pretty soon she and everyone else at Camp 22 would learn to fear him. He would have the respect he deserved.

***

Simon slept for most of the afternoon, rousing himself only when the guard came by tooting on his whistle for an extra roll call. Mal-Chin stayed by his side, propping him up when his injuries left him too exhausted to stand on his own.

Why had the assistant director singled him out? Was it pure and simple bad luck? Or was there more to it? Had Lang read through the records and discovered Simon and Mal-Chin were both Christians? Did he want Simon to betray his friend?

Simon's sentence was already certain. The only thing he didn't know was if his doom would come from the National Security Agency or his own cellmates. If he defied the assistant director's orders, he had no doubt Lang would have him killed. But when his cellmates caught him spying, his fate would prove just as brutal.

That evening, the shrill whistle sounded for yet another roll call. Mal-Chin took him by the elbow, and the three-fingered prisoner stood on his other side to hoist him up. Simon didn't even know the boy's name. He glanced over, and the kid smiled at him. The gesture was simple, and it vanished less than a second after it appeared. Simon tried to guess how old he was. And was he in prison for his own crimes, or those of a distant relative? Simon tried to smile back and knew he couldn't turn his cellmates in.

When night came, he waited until everyone had been asleep for several hours before he slipped the pen and paper out of his waistband. Even though nobody had made any noise, his heart raced. He willed his hands to steady themselves as he carefully unfolded the page. With each rustle of the paper against itself, he held his breath and strained his ears to detect any movement in his cell. The electricity had been turned off, but Simon wouldn't need a light.

The sound of his pen scratching the paper grated against Simon's ears. He grimaced and froze. Nothing stirred. He waited for his pulse to decelerate before he began again. His note to Hannah was longer than he intended, but there was so much he had to tell her. He hoped she could decipher his scribbles. Once he filled the front page, he made the first fold to close it and then stopped. How long had it been since Hannah read the Bible? He thought about her ministering in the infirmary day after day, pouring out her healing and grace to so many. Was she thirsty for the Word of God to fill her back up again? He jotted down a few verses from the Sermon on the Mount, folded the paper up the rest of the way, and hid it inside his waistband.

His only prayer was to get the note to Hannah before the National Security Agency learned of his treason. She had to know how much he loved her.

CHAPTER 30

Officer Lang didn't acknowledge the interruption to his morning schedule until the secretary cleared his throat several times. "What do you want?" Lang finally growled.

The secretary's fingers clenched and unclenched. "I asked the guard for the report, sir. The one from the inmate you recruited."

Lang leaned back in his chair and held out his hand. "Well, let's see it." The secretary hesitated. Lang scowled. "Is there a problem?"

"The prisoner hasn't turned it in yet."

Lang frowned out the window overlooking the infirmary. So, 39846 thought he could flaunt a romance with the infirmary nurse *and* withhold his reports? Not a chance. Lang rose to his feet. "Thank you, Comrade Secretary."

The man didn't seem to know whether to wait for further orders or run out of the office. Watching the boy's indecision was worse than suffering a full-body rash in the heat of summer. Lang waved him away, and the secretary scurried out with a high-pitched, "Yes, sir."

Lang snapped his pencil in half. He didn't really care what was in the reports, but Chief Officer Yeong certainly did. Lang would worry about him later. Now he had more important things to tend to. Like 39846. He stormed down the hall, and several members of his staff had to slide up against the wall to get out of his way. "Get me 39846," he bellowed to the guard as he rounded the last corner. He saw the prisoner as soon as the cells came into view. 39846 was hunched over slightly, his face swollen and bruised. Lang could scarcely stomach the sight of him.

The other prisoners in his cell shrunk toward the back wall, all except a stocky one with a mange of dirty white hair who propped 39846 up by the elbow. "Out of my way, old man," Lang snarled, plowing past the guard who held open the cell door. "This has nothing to do with you."

The elderly prisoner took a barely perceptible step forward. "He's weak, sir. He ..."

Lang struck out once, and the granddad toppled to the ground, like a seedling before a howling wind. Number 39846 glanced down at the old man and flinched. Lang brought his face right up to the prisoner's. "Give me my papers." 39846 looked around, but all of his cellmates had huddled together in the back of the cell. "Your job was to keep track of what went on in here. Now show me your report."

"I haven't written anything down yet." The prisoner's voice was calm, but Lang could smell his nervousness. He would be cowering before this meeting was over.

"You imbecile." Lang's armpits were slimy with perspiration. "What have you written?"

The prisoner lifted one shoulder ever so slightly. That hint of a shrug was enough to make Lang's blood seethe. He grabbed 39846 and yanked his shirt up. Snatching the secret pouch, he broke the belt with one hard jerk. He sensed some kind of uneasy motion from the herd of prisoners in the back, but they were insignificant. His hands trembling with rage, Lang fumbled with the drawstring and untied the pouch. He tugged out the papers and threw one down after another. "You haven't written a single word?"

"I didn't have the chance." There was something of a tremor now in the prisoner's voice.

Lang had just started thinking of how fun it would be to break 39846 right here in front of everybody when he realized something. "You're missing a page."

Now the fearful stink was unmistakable. "That's all I had."

Lang grabbed 39846 by the waistband. A folded piece of paper made a dull little thud when it hit the ground. Lang stooped down. "Secret note?" The corner of his lip curled upward. 39846 shuddered. This was just too good.

With deliberate, dramatic movements, he unfolded the page. "*My dearest beloved.*" Lang let his voice creep up to a discordant falsetto.

The prisoner's whole body tensed. Dread wafted out from every pore.

"*Every dark night I spend here away from you is torture to my soul.*" Lang struck the paper for emphasis. He skimmed several lines down and let his jaw drop open in mock alarm. "What's this?" He pointed to some scribbles on the back. "These wouldn't be Bible verses, would they?" It was hard to conceal his smirk.

39846's expression was etched in granite, but his jaw muscle twitched once.

Lang drew his lips together in a tight line. "That's what I thought. And who did you write this luscious poetry for?" He brought his face so close to the prisoner's he could almost taste his terror-drenched sweat. "Hmmm?"

"I won't tell you anything." The prisoner's voice was low like a growl. He wouldn't be so bold if he knew Lang had discovered his secret weeks ago. The assistant director wondered how far 39846 would let himself be goaded before reacting physically.

"That's your choice." Lang held the incriminating paper tight in his fist. 39846 looked like a wild hare, uncertain if he should stay frozen in its tracks or make a bold dash out of danger. It was that moment of hesitation that made the hunt so exhilarating. Lang brought his lips to the prisoner's ear. "Why don't I take this letter here down to the infirmary and deliver it to your little lover myself?"

39846 snatched the air. Lang took a step back, holding the

page up high where everyone could see. "A love letter for the infirmary nurse," he announced to the entire prison ward. This was working out more beautifully than anything he could have choreographed on his own. "With passages from the incendiary book of Western propaganda!" From the back of the cell, the other inmates kept their eyes to the floor. Lang skimmed more of the letter and pointed to a line. "Should I read this part out loud? This is especially touching."

39846 lunged forward, and Lang shifted his position, purposefully allowing the prisoner's hand to graze his shoulder. "Guards!" he shrieked, and within seconds, two officers were swinging their batons high in the air until 39846's grunting finally died down.

Officer Lang dusted off his hands and strode casually out of the cell. He glanced at his watch and called back to the inmates, "Roll call in twenty minutes. Make sure you're all ready."

***

She stepped up to the bedside of an old woman who was burned in one of the factories. Hannah wrinkled her nose at the scent of charred flesh until she caught her patient staring at her with half-closed eyes. "I dreamed of my daughter."

Trying to conquer her gag reflex, Hannah reached out and stroked her matted hair. "Was it a nice dream?"

A smile pierced the multiple cracks and crevices on the woman's face. "Lovely. We were eating rice together."

"I hope it comes true, then."

The woman's eyes rolled up for a second. "My daughter is dead."

Hannah didn't have a chance to respond before someone spun her around.

"Come with me. Now." The assistant director grabbed her

shoulder. Her body functioned automatically. Her brain went numb. She had known he would come back for her. She wasn't surprised. She couldn't even say she was scared. Just ashamed. Ashamed she wouldn't be strong enough to fight him off. Ashamed of what Simon would think if he found out.

She tripped once, but he dragged her by the arm. He stormed past his office without slowing down, and for the slightest second, she allowed herself to hope. Maybe he was taking her to the administrative ward for a reprimand. Maybe there was an injured patient in another part of the complex who needed her. He rounded the corner to the cells, and then she knew. This wasn't about just her.

"Roll call!" The assistant director's voice was nearly as shrill as the whistle he blew in her ear. Men staggered to their feet and lined up. She glanced toward Simon's cell, and her pulse quickened when she saw the expressions on his comrades' faces. None of them met her gaze. She followed their stares to the ground, where Simon lay in a heap. She hurried ahead.

"Not so fast." This time, the assistant director's voice was more menacing, its characteristic whine replaced by a low, dangerous snarl. His fingers pinched into her arm, and she stopped struggling. She couldn't even tell if Simon was alive or not.

Slowly, one deliberate step after another, the assistant director pushed her forward until she stood directly in front of the bars. "Get him up." An old man with white hair, one of Hannah's former patients from the infirmary, wrapped an arm around Simon and raised him to his feet. Hannah let out her breath when Simon's eyes fluttered open. His face was distorted. Dried blood caked around his mouth. Sticky red pools congealed around multiple wounds on his forehead.

The assistant director shoved Hannah forward. She bit her lip and clenched the bars. "You should be proud of your boyfriend." The assistant director waved a crinkled piece of paper in the air, letting it rustle loudly. "He's quite the poet, you know." He made a show of studying the page. "I even think there's some lines here about you."

She looked at Simon, hardly hearing the assistant director. His eyes met hers, and he blinked. The only thing she wanted was to go to him, clean his wounds, calm his spirit. She fought back her tears.

"*I never imagined I could feel so complete before you walked into my life.*" A few of the prisoners in the other cells chuckled nervously as the assistant director read from Simon's page. He beat the paper with his finger. "And that's not even the half of it. Here on the back." He shoved the letter in front of her face. "Care to guess what's on it?"

Hannah's heart froze over with cold. She felt her body sway from a heaviness she couldn't stop. They had caught Simon with Bible verses. And he was writing to her. Whatever happened to him next, whatever had happened to him already — it was her fault. She let go of the bar, her legs scarcely able to support her weight.

The assistant director motioned for the white-haired man to prop Simon's head up. "Do you know what day tomorrow is, prisoner?" the assistant director growled.

"No, sir," Simon gurgled.

"It's the Day of the Sun." He pointed his bony finger at Simon. "And you and your girlfriend will make a great show to help us commemorate the Eternal President's birthday."

All courage, all stamina, all faith drained out of Hannah's body. She felt it desert her out the soles of her feet and seep through the cold concrete floor.

"She had nothing to do with this." Simon's words were as shaky as Hannah's limbs. "That letter wasn't even meant for her."

"You're a horrible liar," Lang countered.

"Just let her go," Simon tried again, "and then you can make whatever show out of me you want. Tie me up, bury me alive, let me swing from the gallows. It's up to you. I won't fight it. Just let her go back to where she belongs."

"Where she belongs," the assistant director sneered, "is ..." He stopped himself. His voice grew saccharine. "You don't want her to join our little celebration tomorrow in honor of the Eternal President?"

"No."

Goosebumps raced across Hannah's skin. She wanted to warn Simon. Didn't he know he was walking into a trap?

"All right then." The assistant director grabbed her by the arm, pinching her bicep. "You wouldn't let me have you," he snarled. "Let's see how long you last in there with all them."

Hannah's legs buckled, and the assistant director had to support all her weight. She fixed her eyes on Simon, whose pupils had widened in horror.

After fumbling with the lock, the assistant director threw her into the cell. She landed on her elbows. "Have fun, men," he called out. "And remember, 39846 doesn't want her to die tomorrow so, well ... you'd better be thorough and finish the job for me. Think of this as my early Day of the Sun gift to you all. "

The white-haired prisoner reached down to her. "I'd stay out of the way, old man." The assistant director chuckled. "The younger ones will want to have their turn first."

Simon coughed weakly. "You won't touch her ..." Blood and saliva dribbled down from his mouth. He spat on the floor. "None of you will lay a hand on her."

Lang spun on his heel. He threw a set of the keys to the guard. "Call me when they're through."

CHAPTER 31

Simon didn't have any strength left, but he would die before he let one of his cellmates harm her. As soon as Lang was gone, he sank to the floor beside her. She scampered toward him like a rodent scurrying from a predator. He held her as she trembled, felt her body heave with sobs, and tried to shelter her from the other prisoners' view, praying God would let him protect her one last time.

He squeezed his eyes shut and tried to envelop as much of her body as he could so whatever blows that came would land on him instead of her. He pictured his cellmates inching their way closer, sharing looks, deciding who would lead in the attack. Simon knew he wouldn't last long. "I'm sorry," he whispered to Hannah in advance.

A hand on his shoulder made him jump. He tightened his hold on Hannah. "It's me, Brother." Mal-Chin stretched out both hands and nodded at the other prisoners. "Nobody's going to hurt your friend."

Simon let out his breath but didn't let go. The boy with three fingers shuffled forward. "It was brave of you not to report on us. Brave and dumb." He dipped his head by way of compliment, and Simon stared wide-eyed.

Another prisoner came forward and tapped Hannah on the shoulder. Her head was buried in Simon's chest, and he felt all her air suck in at the touch. Simon angled his shoulder to try to shield her.

"I just wanted to see if she remembered me," the young man

explained. "She took care of me when I got frostbite. I wanted to say thank you is all."

Simon eased his posture and stroked Hannah's hair. Her muscles didn't relax. "Give them a little privacy," Mal-Chin muttered, and the men ambled awkwardly away.

Simon didn't know what to say. He felt Hannah's heart flutter against his chest. He tipped her chin up to his. She lowered her gaze and tried to hide, but he stroked her cheek and tilted her face up again. He longed to kiss her cracked lips, to cover her with his love until all her scars and injuries vanished. She hadn't stopped trembling. He rested his chin on the top of her head and prayed. If God was merciful, he would let them both die right now. But this was no fairy tale. No matter how fervent his prayers, no matter how deep his love, Camp 22 was no place for happy endings.

**

Officer Lang took a sip of tepid coffee and leaned back in his chair. He smacked his lips noisily and thought about how the little flirt from the infirmary had resisted him right here on this desk. Memories that previously humiliated and infuriated him now erupted into a self-satisfied grin. She didn't want to give in to him. He'd see how she handled herself with a dozen hardened culprits. Some of those men hadn't touched a woman in years. Now she'd realize what sort of mistake she'd made rejecting him.

He exhaled loudly and congratulated himself. The letter he discovered was enough to warrant 39846's immediate execution. The Christian pig would make a worthy spectacle for the Day of the Sun. Lang leaned back in his chair. When he saw his secretary dart past, he pounded on the window and beckoned him in. The young man scurried to the doorway, bowing as he entered.

Lang smirked. "Call up the Chief Officer. Tell Yeong he'll

have his demonstration tomorrow."

***

Hannah burrowed her head into Simon's chest, and even though he couldn't see her face, he had already memorized the exact location of each cut and bruise. *A little more time, God,* he begged. *A little more time with her.*

Simon was a dead man. Disobeying direct orders, copying Bible verses, hiding a romantic relationship with another prisoner ... Simon couldn't even count all the crimes he had committed against the National Security Agency. He wouldn't regret dying himself, but he was a fool for writing her that letter. He was stupid to think a love like theirs could flourish undetected. And why had he included those Bible passages? What idiocy had possessed him to risk her life like that? He could only guess what Lang would do when he came back and found her unharmed. Maybe they could find a way to conceal her before he arrived. Simon was off to the scaffold or the firing squad no matter what happened. He just wished he could find a way to spare Hannah from the same fate. He rubbed his cheek against her hair. How could heaven contain anything more beautiful? "I'm sorry."

"For what?" She glanced up. The bruises on her face brought him more pain than the torturer's chair.

"For not doing a better job protecting you."

Hannah kissed his fingers, which had intertwined with hers. "I never wanted you to protect me." She reached up and brushed his forehead. "I only wanted to be with you."

"I didn't think it would turn out like this." It was a foolish confession. They had slipped uninvited into North Korea. What else should he have expected? There were times during his detainment downstairs when all he hoped for was death. But now, now that she was here with him, his lungs constricted, gasping for a freedom he longed for more passionately than he could express with words.

He sniffed and pulled her even more tightly to him. "I would have made you my wife, you know." His throat nearly gave out. "You would have been such a beautiful ..." His voice caught again, and his tears wet Hannah's cheek. "Such a beautiful mother." Now he had started, he couldn't stop himself. "When I had that fever, I watched you in the infirmary every day, watched the way you cared for the sick, the way they loved you and you loved them. And I imagined what it would be like if we ever got out of here, if God let us marry. Start a family. I even had a dream one night. It was you and me, and we had a little baby girl ..."

"Stop." The agony in her voice matched the intensity of his own emotions. His chest squeezed tight, but he had to tell her the rest. He couldn't stop now.

"You were singing to her. It was the most beautiful hymn." He coughed. "I could still hear how you sang it when I woke up. When things were at their worst, I just thought about your voice. It was perfect. Like heaven." His tears were flowing freely. He didn't wipe them away. "And one day, I woke up, and I couldn't remember what your voice sounded like anymore." A pinching, suffocating anguish gripped his heart. "I couldn't remember your singing." He leaned his head against her shoulder, his body heaving with silent sobs.

Hannah's voice was so quiet that she was already past the second line before he realized what she was doing. He glanced around. Prisoners stopped shuffling and stared.

"I love thee in life, I will love thee in death and praise thee as long as thou lendest me breath."

Her song wavered through the silence and grew louder as her confidence increased.

"And sing when the death-dew lies cold on my brow, 'If ever I love thee, my Jesus, 'tis now.'"

Was this what heaven would sound like? Was God giving him a taste of eternity to give him courage for what was to come?

"In mansions of glory and endless delight ..."

He shut his eyes. This couldn't be real. A beauty this poignant couldn't thrive in the midst of such gruesome squalor.

"I'll ever adore thee in heaven so bright."

He didn't want to let out his breath. The song was so delicate, so surreal he feared a single movement might break its spell.

"And sing with the glittering crown on my brow, 'If ever I loved thee, my Jesus, 'tis now.'"

After the last note reverberated against the cell walls, it was still several seconds before he dared to breathe again. How could the angels worship God in heaven while Hannah was still here on earth? If her countenance grew any more radiant, she would be visibly glowing. He was still holding her in his arms, or else he wouldn't believe she was flesh and blood.

The entire prison complex was silent. Even the guard gawked. The men in his own cell had dispersed against the walls, as if they recognized the holiness of the moment and didn't want to intrude. Simon breathed in the smell of Hannah's grimy hair. He couldn't let the assistant director come and take her away. His own life was forfeit, but before he died, he needed to find a way to get her out of here. He pressed his fingers against his throbbing temples. He had to focus.

"You don't need to worry about me, you know." Hannah's whisper dissolved the aura of serenity and peace her song had cast over the complex. She laid her hand on his shoulder. She shouldn't be here. None of this should be happening. Where was Moses? Where was the deliverance Simon had dreamed about? Where was God's mercy? Simon didn't mind dying. He was ready to leave this prison cell for good. But Hannah ... How could someone with such a charitable spirit be condemned to such a fate as this? *She still has work to fulfill, Lord. Take me if you will, but please spare her.*

He wished she didn't look so tranquil. It made the impossibility of their situation that much more difficult to accept. "I'll get you out of here," Simon mumbled into the dirt.

She grazed his cheek with her finger. "You've looked out for me long enough." Her words were gentle, soft, but they pierced through his heart like a jagged-edged knife. "My future is in God's hands."

He couldn't speak for fear his voice would betray his fears, his despair. He had to be strong. There had to be some way.

"At least we have one more night together." She squeezed his hand.

It was too much for Simon. "We have to do something." He stood up and balled his fists, turning to his colleagues. "We can't let Lang come back and take her."

CHAPTER 32

Hannah sat back and listened while Simon talked to the other prisoners in his cell. They huddled near the back corner, and even though they probably thought they were keeping their voices down, she could hear every word.

"We won't just hand her over to him."

"What else can we do?"

"There's one assistant director and twelve of us. If we all work together ..."

Hannah stood. She had heard enough. "No." She made her way to the huddle.

Simon drew her toward him with his arm around her waist. "We were just trying to ..."

"Stop it." She reached up and swept away some of the hair that had clumped to the dried blood on his forehead. "No one else is getting hurt."

"I know," Simon crooned, but Hannah doubted he really understood at all. The whole time she spent in Yanji, she had been singled out because she was a girl. Several other girls started the Secret Seminary training with her, but within a few months, Hannah was the only one remaining. The Sterns reminded her at least once a day how special she was since she stuck with the program. Did Simon and Levi and the rest of the students get that kind of attention? No. Only Hannah. Why? Because she was a girl. Simon had followed her, put himself in danger for her, botched his entire mission just for her. Because she was a girl. At the safe house in Sanhe, she had lost count of how many times Mr. Kim or

Kwan expressed shock that Moses had chosen her ... because she was a girl. And now, a dozen strangers were talking about throwing their lives away to protect her from a man with the full force of the National Security Agency behind him.

All because she was a girl.

"We want to help you." Simon wiped the tear that streaked down her face.

He didn't understand at all. He probably thought she was crying out of fear. He had no idea how ashamed she was right now to be a woman, to be the sort of creature who would inspire men to sacrifice their lives for no reason whatsoever. If she could strip off her sex and die with these men as an equal, she would lift her head proudly and stare her executioners right in the eye. But she was only a girl. A girl no man was going to risk his life for.

"I'll handle the assistant director when he comes back," Hannah stated, but she doubted Simon and the others even heard her.

***

"So what are we going to do?" the three-fingered youth asked. "He'll be coming back for her any minute, you know."

Simon felt Hannah's muscles seize up next to him. He wished the men wouldn't talk about the assistant director. He glanced at her blackened eye and felt his blood pressure rise at the mere thought of anyone who would want to hurt her. *Lord, just show us what to do.* Was God even listening? Why wasn't he acting? If anyone deserved a chance to live out her calling, it was Hannah. *I don't care what you let them do to me, Lord, but please show us a way to free her.*

He leaned his head down and breathed in the soft scent of her hair. It was a different smell than what he remembered from Yanji, when they were able to bathe regularly and wash with the

Americans' artificially-scented soaps and shampoos. But it was still her. And Simon would rather die than see her come to any harm.

He shut his eyes for a moment. Was there really no escape for her? He always imagined he might one day face a martyr's death. He never pictured Hannah sharing that fate with him. He thought about the night they both left Yanji, the hours he spent following her, the way she clung to him in the woods, the feel of her heart fluttering against his chest. How much had changed since then. Even now with his injuries, he guessed he could pick her up with one arm for all the weight she had lost at Camp 22.

He didn't realize his vision was blurry until she looked up at him with a serene smile. "Your friends don't need to rescue me. I'm ready to go home. We'll meet the Lord together."

Simon swallowed. He wasn't ready to give up yet. He held Hannah a little tighter. How long until the assistant director came and took her away forever? What tortures and humiliations would he dream up when he found the prisoners hadn't carried out his plans? This was Simon's last chance to wrap Hannah up in his arms, his last chance to tell her how adored she was. Did she even realize how much he loved her? How could he sit back and let the assistant director just steal her away from him?

Hannah tugged on his sleeve and led him away from the circle. Nobody said anything as they left. He wiped his cheek with the back of his hand.

Hannah lowered herself to the ground, pulling him softly down next to her. "We only have a little more time. We shouldn't waste it."

He shook his head. "There must be something we can do."

"You know, I sometimes prayed for the Lord to allow such an event. For us to go home together."

Simon's throat felt like he had swallowed a cupful of glass. "You're not going home yet."

She placed her palm on his shoulder. His body was trembling. He wanted to say something more. She was wrong. She wouldn't die. She couldn't. But he had no voice, no words. He kissed the top of her head. She didn't understand. He could face whatever the National Security Agency could dream up for him as long as she survived, as long as she stayed safe, as long as she could keep leading people to salvation, as long as she could keep healing others with her kind and compassionate touch.

She looked up at him. Didn't she realize, didn't she know that he only had one real fear — the fear of failing her again? He would die a hundred times if it would save her. He would gladly trade his life for her freedom. She could go back to Yanji, she could go on to South Korea or the United States. She could fulfill her destiny as a gracious Christian saint. Simon shook his head. It was a futile hope, just like his dreams of one day marrying her. He wouldn't live past tomorrow.

In reality, she probably wouldn't, either.

Her body felt as thin as paper pressed up against him. He wondered if they would be able to share this same kind of closeness in heaven or if this was their last embrace. If there was any chance they might escape and free themselves of the National Security Agency, he would risk anything to stay with her. But all hope had deserted him, and in its place was only a heavy, unshakeable resignation. He took her hand and gave it a small squeeze. "I wish there was something I could do."

Her whole face shined. "I just want you to love me."

How could his spirit survive this torture? How could his soul endure such agony? "You know I always have." He swallowed, but that did nothing to relieve the lump in the back of his throat. "And I always will."

***

Lang threw his clipboard on the table, relishing the discordant sound of metal clanking against metal. The Chief Officer of Productivity would have himself a demonstration to remember for decades to come. Lang had already ordered the extra rations for the prisoners. Even the politically corrupt would fill their bellies tomorrow. They would feast on the Eternal President's birthday. Of course, Lang had to warn his guards to keep watch. Contented stomachs could lead to unrest. When the prisoners were kept just one crumb away from starvation, revolt was impossible. Well, it didn't matter. His demonstration tomorrow would scare even the tiniest trace of disloyalty or rebellion out of these criminals. A Christian pig shot in front of everyone …

But why stop at one execution? Lang checked his watch. Perhaps if he got to her in time, it could still be a double demonstration — two Christian traitors tried and killed together. He had a feeling that behind Officer Yeong's sober, stoic exterior lay an appreciation for the dramatic. How long had he left her in there? There was no reason for haste. A few more minutes couldn't hurt. If she died too soon, Lang could always find some others to kill off alongside 39846. And if she was still alive, well, he didn't want to rush the prisoners. After all, the Day of the Sun was an occasion for generosity. Why not let the men enjoy their little diversion a while longer? Lang smiled and pictured the regret on the infirmary nurse's face when she realized what a pitiful, fatal mistake she had made when she refused him. Let them have their fun just a quarter of an hour more. She'd die one way or the other. However it played out, Lang would get his revenge. And the Chief Officer would get his demonstration.

***

It was his last night with Hannah. He didn't want to waste it sleeping. Her head rested on the crook of his elbow. She was so peaceful. So tender. He held her fragile body with both arms, unable to stop wondering what would happen when the assistant director returned. Simon leaned down and nuzzled her ear with his nose, his fear of losing her surpassed only by the intensity of his love. At least God gave him this one last chance to hold her before he died.

In another universe, they would be married by now. Maybe even have a baby. Hannah would make such a patient, gentle mother. But that was another world. Another place. Not the future God had ordained for either of them. How strange he had never been afraid to die until he held her in his arms.

"You know I'd marry you if I could," he admitted. She didn't say anything, and he figured she must be asleep. "The minute I found us a minister, I would make you my wife. I'd wake you up with a kiss every morning, and stay up at night just so I could watch you sleep. I would pro ..." His voice faltered. He sniffed. "I would protect you." A single tear splashed down on her forearm. He brushed it away, his fingers soaking in the warmth of her skin.

"Marry me," she whispered.

There was no reason to be ashamed. Not in front of her. Not when the assistant director had already signed their death warrants. Twenty-four hours from now, he wouldn't even be alive to regret his rash confession. "I mean it." He pressed his forehead against hers. "I'd marry you the moment we were free."

"No." Her voice was so soft, he had to lean farther down to hear her better. "Marry me now."

He clutched her so tight his arms shook. "You know if there was any way ..."

"We only have a few minutes left."

"But there isn't any minister to ..."

"I'll do it."

Simon jumped at the voice. For the briefest moment, it had been so easy to imagine he and Hannah were totally alone. Mal-Chin stood above them, with an awkward, almost embarrassed smile on his wrinkled face.

"I'm sorry for interrupting, but I overheard. And I can imagine no higher honor than joining you two in marriage."

CHAPTER 33

At any minute, Simon expected Mal-Chin or Hannah or maybe both of them to burst out laughing. Marriage? When his execution was scheduled for tomorrow? When Lang was due to come back any minute and tear Hannah away from him forever? A dozen protests ran through his head, but all Simon said was, "But you aren't a minister."

Mal-Chin pointed to the glaring bald scar on his head he got the night the guards raided their secret meeting. He stretched out the collar of his prison uniform to reveal a puncture wound on his shoulder nearly two centimeters in diameter. "If these don't qualify me as a minister, nothing will."

Hannah held onto Simon's arm, stroking his bicep with those gentle, gracious fingers. That touch ... How could he leave her behind? Now that he had held her, kissed her, how could he let her go forever? They should be plotting her escape, not their nuptials. Simon looked away, straining his ears to hear the assistant director's footsteps. The plan would never work. Lang would arrive any minute, and then what? He pressed his fingers against his throbbing temples. There must be some way to get her out of here ...

"Are you ready?" Hannah's breath on his ear dragged Simon away from thoughts of escape, of the assistant director, of freedom or executions. They evaporated into the darkness like a mist. He couldn't find his voice.

He wanted to tell her how beautiful she was. He wanted to tell her she was more precious than any earthly jewel. But all he could manage to stammer was, "You realize that tomorrow ..."

She ended his argument with a kiss. When Simon opened his eyes, he saw Mal-Chin trying to hide a grin. "Let's scoot a little further back, children." Mal-Chin nodded to the guard on watch. "Further away from that light."

Hannah took his hand and leaned her head on Simon's shoulder as they drifted into the shadows.

"You know how long I've wanted to do this?" he asked.

"I do."

They stopped when they reached the wall and looked to Mal-Chin. "I can think of no better way to start this most blessed, most unusual marriage than to pray and ask our Father for his ..."

A light flickered on the ceiling. *No,* Simon groaned inwardly. *Not yet. Please, not yet.* Hannah tightened her grip on his hand but said nothing.

Mal-Chin's gaze flashed to the side, but he quickly cleared his throat. "Actually, let's pray after. Simon, do you vow before God to always ..."

"Where is she?" The nasally voice was unmistakable. Simon felt Hannah's hand go completely cold. "What's happened to her?"

"... cherish and protect Hannah, to enter into the holy covenant of marriage, to love her with ..."

"I do," Simon blurted. *Dear Jesus, I do. Now please, just give us another minute longer.*

"What do you mean, nothing happened?" Lang raged. "She's been here over an hour!"

Jesus, no. Simon felt Hannah's legs start to give way. He caught her just as a flashlight beam captured them both. "I'm so sorry, my love," he whispered.

As a key clanged in the lock, she glanced up at him. Her lip quivered, but her voice was firm. "I love you. I won't ever stop loving you."

The assistant director yanked her by the hair. She grimaced

but didn't cry out. "So they were too afraid to touch you, were they? Too afraid to insult the honor of a ..."

Something rumbled deep within Simon's gut, and he leapt on the assistant director's back.

"No, Brother." He heard Mal-Chin's voice but ignored the old man's pleas. He scratched at the assistant director's face. His only thoughts were of murder. Lang screamed and hurled him off. Simon landed on his back with a heavy thud. Hannah's voice made a tiny little squeak that reminded Simon how weak his own body was.

Mal-Chin squatted down beside him. "Are you hurt, Brother?" The question didn't warrant a reply. Hannah was to the front of the cell now. The guard held open the door so the assistant director could steal her away. Simon tried to prop himself up. If he could find his breath, he just might ...

"Let her go." Mal-Chin laid a strong hand on Simon's shoulder. Hannah's blurry form disappeared around the corner. Simon wanted to call out to her, but couldn't find his voice. Mal-Chin leaned down and whispered in his ear, "She's in the good Lord's hands."

Simon couldn't tell if he was blinded by tears or sheer fury. He sat up, and a visceral, animal-like wail welled up from the depths of his gut. He opened his mouth to scream, but no sound emerged. The entire cell was silent except for Mal-Chin crooning, "All we can do is pray, Brother. All we can do is pray."

***

Surrounded by darkness, Hannah couldn't remember if the assistant director had beaten her or not. She couldn't remember if she had screamed or fought back or maybe even blacked out as he dragged her downstairs to the solitary confinement cells. She recounted as much of the past day as she could and guessed it was night. Still, the darkness here could lie. She knew she had been with Simon. The memory of his warmth lingered on her skin, on her hand, on her cheek. Her forearm tingled where his fingers had caressed her.

There was something about a wedding. It felt so real, or had she just dreamed it? How long ago had the assistant director thrown her down here? Aside from a little soreness on her arm, she didn't think she was injured. But what if she just couldn't remember? Even worse, what if she woke up tomorrow and realized she had never been with Simon at all?

Her breathing grew faster. She reached out her arms. Were the walls moving closer? Once she overheard a guard taunt a prisoner with threats of a shrinking cell. The walls just kept on closing in, one deadly centimeter at a time. *Jesus.* Hannah couldn't pray any further than that. Why was she down here? Why back in solitary? Both sets of fingertips brushed against the cold walls. So the cell really was caving in. Or had it always been this small? *Dear God,* she prayed again, but there was no answer.

"Simon!" Her voice sounded shrill and foreign. She tried to stop her body from shaking. "Simon!" The echo was nearly deafening. She buried her head in her hands, hands she knew had just recently clutched his. But how could she be sure? A needle. The assistant director had come at her with a needle. She had scratched his face. *Help me, Jesus.* She tried to recall what happened before he threw her down here. *Simon, where are you? What's happening to me?*

She fingered her sore forearm and rocked her body back and forth. She bumped her head once. Did that mean the ceiling was getting lower too? No. A concrete box didn't shrink all by itself. So why was it so cramped? *Light.* She needed light. Even the slightest trace, just to convince her she was in her own right body. She hadn't already died, had she? When the assistant director jabbed her with the needle, at first she thought it was poison. She had kicked him. Scratched at him. She couldn't die yet. Simon needed her. She recalled the assistant director's sneer just as clearly as if he were still standing in front of her, but she couldn't remember what he did to her. *God, just help me remember. Is Simon even alive? Am I?*

She called out into the darkness. "Help me, please!" A slight breeze tickled her sweaty neck. "Is somebody in here?" She stretched out her arms but felt only the wall. There wasn't room in this cage for two. She was imagining things again. Something the assistant director gave her ...

"My little one is struggling to find the peace her soul craves." The voice was ancient and craggy. Hannah strained her ears. She wanted Simon. She needed Simon. Where was he?

"The Lord Almighty, the Great Comforter, can bring you the rest you thirst for." A hand like the wind swept some hair across her brow. When Hannah reached up, it vanished, but the voice remained. "My little one has come to the end of a long and terrifying journey." Hannah squinted, trying to pierce through the blinding darkness. "On the other side, you and your beloved will be reunited, but not before you pass the Great Waters."

"Who are you?" Hannah's body had stopped trembling, and she felt drowsy. Was any of this real? Could this whole ordeal just be some kind of nightmare? Would she wake up tomorrow in Yanji, go downstairs, and tell Simon about her crazy dream?

"Peace, little one. Your voyage is long and dangerous. May the rich blessings and protection of our God and Father cover you, and may the blood of Christ preserve you from all harm."

Hannah couldn't keep her eyes open. A melody lilted somewhere in the distance. If she strained all of her attention, she thought she might be able to make it out, but she was too tired. Oh, so tired. She let out a long breath.

The voice was quieter now, far off and fading like the music itself. "We'll meet again, little one. I will look for you there with your husband."

Husband. The word was so quiet she could scarcely hear it, but it infused Hannah with a surge of clarity. She remembered now. The almost-wedding. The Day of the Sun. The assistant director's threats. Her lungs refused to draw air.

Tomorrow, Simon would die.

Why him? She thought about when she first left Yanji, how terrified she was to never know what happened to him. Now she realized how stupid she had been. If she didn't know where he was, there was at least the hope he was safe. But that chance was gone to her now. Tomorrow, he would be dead. All her impossible notions, her senseless fantasies would die with him. She thought back on all those sleepless nights, all the energy she wasted daydreaming of things that could never be. Tomorrow he would die, but that didn't make her stop loving him today. It didn't make her hands stop sweating or her stomach stop somersaulting at the recollection of his touch. It didn't erase her memory of his whispers in the darkness.

She had always known it could never be. Hannah squeezed her eyes shut. Hot tears pooled in the corners, tears that nobody would ever see or care about. Tears that wasted water and energy, but that refused to stay in place.

A few hours ago, she had almost become a bride. Tomorrow, she would be nothing more than an unmarried widow.

CHAPTER 34

When the lights came on that morning, Simon was still awake, slouched down against the wall. In a few hours, it would all be over. At some point last night after Hannah was taken away, he stopped thinking about the afterlife. All he wanted was for his time on earth to end. His soul was a void, free from pain, free from joy, free from hope.

"You didn't sleep, Brother?" Mal-Chin lowered himself to the ground beside him. Simon heard the syllables of his friend's words, could vaguely piece together their meaning, but had no response.

The guard sounded his whistle, and the prisoners leapt to attention. Simon wondered vaguely why his body still obeyed that sharp, shrill call. What could they do to him now if he disobeyed? What else could they take from him? Even torture had lost the terror it once held. His life was already forfeit, ripped away from him, soon to be discarded forever.

Officer Lang strode in, spine erect. Simon's gut twisted in place. He looked for some sign of smugness on the assistant director's face, some clue so he could guess what happened to Hannah last night. All he noticed were the bulging veins in Lang's neck. The assistant director scowled and pointed at him. "You there. Get moving."

Simon's legs submitted to the order, and as he walked away from his cell, he wondered if the fear would catch up to him at some point before his execution. He glanced back once, not because he wanted a last look at his fellow inmates, but because it somehow seemed expected. Mal-Chin's face was tight and stern as Lang cuffed Simon's wrists. Simon imagined there was some secret message, some hidden word conveyed in his friend's eyes, but couldn't guess what it might be.

The assistant director tugged on his shackles. Simon dragged himself along, and for the first time in recent memory, he was completely pain-free. Had his nervous system already shut itself down? He focused on his breathing just to be sure his lungs still drew air. He sensed the stares of the men as he walked by their cages. Did they pity him? Envy him, perhaps? How many times had he prayed for a swift sentence like this? But that was before. Before he felt her touch once more. Before he held her in his arms. Before he confessed his love to her and nearly made her his bride. His soul was bound heavenward, but his heart was anchored firmly to the squalid, grimy earth.

They passed the spot in the hall where he first kissed her, but no flutters overcame him in that dark corner. He tried but couldn't even recall the sensation of her lips on his. If he had known it would only end in death, could that kiss have made him feel so alive?

They had to walk by the infirmary on their way out. The patients were too sick to notice him marching to his slaughter, but he still felt himself on exhibition. He looked for her, suddenly realizing with dread he might never see her again. For an instant, a brief fleeting second, a surge of strength coursed through his veins, and he imagined breaking free of his restraints. He would fight off the assistant director, find her, and together they would make their suicide dash for freedom. God was a God of miracles. Hadn't Peter and John escaped from their prison? But then, as quickly as it came, the urge passed. His shoulders slouched down, his wrists chaffed against his metal cuffs, and all his remaining energy leaked out through his pores.

So this is what it's like, Simon thought. *This is how it feels to die.*

***

She woke, surprised she had been able to sleep at all. She remembered praying for Simon for hours, begging God to give him strength to face his execution. But now she had no idea what time it was. Was it morning already? Her breath caught, and her heart pounded high up in her chest. Had she slept through the demonstration? Unless someone brought her word, how would she ever know?

She pressed her lips together and clenched her eyes shut. How did God expect her to endure such uncertainty? The tortures she faced at the Chongjin jail were mere child's play compared to this emotional torment. She was jealous of Simon. At least his suffering would be over soon, if it wasn't already. Would he be able to see her from heaven?

It wasn't right for her to complain. She should be happy for Simon, happy God had called him home. But what about her? When would her time come? Up until now, she had always thought of martyrdom as a Christian's highest privilege, reserved only for the most worthy. So had Simon passed the test, and she had somehow failed it? She thought of all the prisoners who died under her care in the infirmary. Had she neglected to tell enough of them the good news of salvation? Had Simon proved himself more faithful than she? Was that why God was bringing him home, leaving her here alone in the dark to mourn?

She didn't recognize the guard who shuffled in. "They're ready for you now." He spoke slowly, but Hannah couldn't tell if that was from reluctance or just indifference.

"Ready?" Her body was poised in limbo. She didn't know if she should recoil in fear of some new sort of torture she was about to endure, or if something else entirely was going on. Maybe God hadn't forgotten her down here after all. Maybe it was all a mistake, Simon and the Eternal President's birthday and the execution. The guard lifted her by the elbow.

"Where are we going?" she asked.

"Assistant director's orders. You're coming to the exhibit for the Day of the Sun."

Hannah's body moved forward, and she tested the news in her mind. At least she would see him one last time. At least she could pray for him as he breathed his last. *God, give me strength.* She swallowed once and checked her voice before using it. "Is everyone in the underground detainment center to witness the execution?"

"No." The guard cleared his throat. Hannah could almost feel his embarrassment diffusing out from his neck and ears. "You're to be part of the exhibit."

"Me?" Could he hear the smile in her words? Could he guess the relief flooding over her at such news?

His gesture was a mix between a shrug and a nod. She followed him down the hall, surprised he didn't bind her. Did he know she had no reason to run? Did he know these last steps brought her closer toward life and toward the one she loved?

She would join Simon. What more could she ask for? Her heart began to swell, swell with love for Simon, with love for her Savior, even with love for the poor boy in front of her who blushed when he delivered the news of her death. The guards here were no different than the inmates, she realized. Both were trapped, both were slaves to the regime, both had been designed for so much more than a place like Camp 22. As each moment brought her nearer to eternity, pity grew in her heart for the National Security agents. Did they stay awake at night, plagued by guilt? Did they also dream of freedom? Her time on earth had been short compared to most, but it had been blessed abundantly. Her only wish...

Hannah took a deep breath. No. This was her homecoming. She didn't want to meet the Almighty with sadness or remorse.

A tear sneaked down her cheek. She thought again about the

guards and officers, the assistant director, the executioner she was about to meet. Their lost souls were worthy of her tears. But him ... Hannah hung her head and bit her quivering lip. If only there was a way to forget her silly, romantic dreams. Forget how passionately she had once hoped. She had no right to question God's plans.

The morning was overcast, but still Hannah blinked in the glaring light when she stepped outside. She raised her hands to her brow to block out the radiance. Mr. Stern once told her mortals couldn't see God or they would be killed immediately by his splendor. Hannah wondered if her first moment in heaven would be painful like this, like stepping into the sun after being trapped for a lifetime in the dark.

A sizable crowd had already assembled near the administration building, and more guards and prisoner units joined the undulating throng from every side. "This way." She could barely hear the man who led her. She lifted her eyes once and glanced around for Simon. Would he be here waiting? Would they have a chance to speak to one another before the end? For the first time that morning, fear pierced through her heart like a National Security agent's bullet. What if Simon wasn't there? What if he somehow convinced the guards he was no longer a threat? What if he denied his faith? After all they had been through together, after everything that passed between them, would he desert her now?

Her heart was pounding by the time she reached the small platform in front of the crowd. Like a hooked fish gasping for air, she darted her eyes back and forth in search of his familiar face. Her breath stuck somewhere in the middle of her throat.

Simon wasn't there.

CHAPTER 35

Simon's wrists were already bleeding by the time Lang dragged him out of the detainment center and toward the administration building. He could hardly feel his legs but stumbled along, tripping regularly, barely able to sense where his feet were in relation to the rest of him. Camp 22's Chief Officer was already addressing the crowds when the throng of prisoners came into view, a gray mass against the backdrop of a drab, cloudy day. "It is the joyful, patriotic duty of every member of this great nation to commemorate the birthday of our beloved Eternal President, who saved us from Western aggressors and constantly provided for us out of his own benevolence and extreme generosity."

Simon thought back to his own childhood, when he had sung songs of Kim Il-Sung's preeminence with as much passion as the rest of his peers. He should be grateful to finally be free of the regime. A few more minutes, and he would never have to hear another propaganda speech again. Soon, the only songs he would sing would be praises of the one true King. He should be ecstatic, leaping and dancing for joy. But his wrists were chaffed and bloody, and after he stepped outside, the arthritic burning in his hips and back only intensified each time he stumbled.

"Hurry up," Lang ordered. Simon gritted his teeth. A few more minutes. Just a little longer, and he would be free.

The speaker cleared his throat. "It is no secret that our nation has struggled arduously at the hands of Imperialist aggressors. But for metal to be perfected, it must first be purified in the furnace, purged of all impurities. It is in this spirit of sacrifice, this spirit of purging, that we bring forth our condemned."

A low cheer sounded, not the lustful howl of the bloodthirsty, but the resigned compliance of the exhausted masses.

"We're late." The assistant director swore and shoved several prisoners out of his way in one sweeping motion.

Simon glanced up. He no longer needed to beg his legs to function. He tried to run, nearly outpacing Lang himself.

There on the platform, biting her cheek and straining her neck, stood Hannah.

***

She let out her breath, and relief washed over her entire being. He was there. He had come. She would not die alone. He was bruised and beaten, but she saw in his eyes that he was ready. As was she.

A lifetime of conversations passed between them in a single moment — the theological discussions they would never have, the sweet musings they would never whisper in the hammock of Mrs. Stern's garden. And in that moment, Hannah knew. She was his, she had always been his. In any other place, any other world, they would have been together already. Simon stepped up on the platform. The droning of the political speech, the shuffling of the prisoners fell mute. It was him, and it was her, and in that moment, she knew everything was exactly as it should be.

Neither of them spoke. They didn't need to. She took a deep breath, thankful for the simple gift of crisp, fresh air. She tore her eyes away from him to glance up at the storm clouds overhead. She prayed for rain to wash their blood off the platform when it was all over. *Lord, send a deluge.* Something rumbled in her spirit. For a moment, she envisioned the entire mass of prisoners of Camp 22 lifting up holy hands in praise and worship of the

Almighty King. She pictured a day — years in the future, but coming nonetheless — when God would transform the very land they stood on. She saw the ground itself purged and cleansed from all the innocent blood it had soaked up over the decades. Former guards and former prisoners met together, clasping hands and asking God to heal and forgive their nation. God answered with torrents of blessings, a flood of his Spirit. The rain would come. Hannah wouldn't be alive to witness it, so God had given her a glimpse of Korea's future glory now.

Mr. Stern's voice whispered to her on a breeze. *"The blood of the martyrs is the seed of the church."* And now she understood. If in some way her death could pave the way for such an outpouring of the Holy Spirit, she would face the sword or the revolver or the gallows a hundred times over. She turned back to Simon. Had he seen it too? Did he know what power and majesty would one day be revealed right here where they stood? Did he understand what an honor it was for God to allow them to meet their end like this — together?

Joy welled up from the core of her being, so irresistible she would have probably started singing right there if the man speaking hadn't looked directly at her. Her spirit already soared heavenward, but her body faltered for a moment. She felt blood drain from her face and willed herself to remember this man too was loved by God.

Father, don't desert me now.

She hadn't even ended her prayer when glorious singing deafened her ears. The music was clearer, purer than anything she had ever listened to, yet it was somehow familiar. Had she heard it in her sleep, maybe? Or in the quietness of Mrs. Stern's garden as she meditated on God's goodness? For the first time, Hannah finally understood the word *homecoming*. This wasn't death, but birth. Birth into a glorious new world without pain or sorrow or terror. No more darkness. No more starvation or trembling. No more heartache. She never knew how much her life was missing until she stood here, so close to eternity. The bullet wouldn't hurt. As long as the music still filled her soul, she doubted she would even feel it.

She was going home.

She stared into the speaker's frowning face and wondered how anyone could stay deaf to the majestic melody. Her eyes passed over the crowds, the prisoners assembled to witness her martyrdom. If only God unplugged their ears, the revival would start right now. Today. If only ...

***

She looked beautiful, like a princess about to address her people. Simon's knees shook. She was too young. A lump lodged in his throat. She deserved so much more than this.

The speaker listed all of Hannah's crimes. Simon stared out across the sea of bodies that stretched out in all directions. So they would kill her first. How could Simon stand by while the executioner pointed his rifle and ripped her life away? How could he stand by and do nothing? Had he even known what fear was before now? Had he even tasted grief? Hannah stood only a few steps away, a radiant smile lighting her perfect, bruised face. Why was she happy? Didn't she know what would happen as soon as the Chief Officer of Productivity finished speaking?

Why, Lord? Why? Why Hannah? Wasn't Simon's sacrifice enough? What had Hannah ever done? She was the most gentle, selfless creature he had ever met. How could the National Security Agency ...

She stared at him. Her eyes were imploring. What was she trying to say? There was such a depth to her expression. *What is it, Hannah? What are you trying to tell me?*

A guard tied her hands behind her back. How could she be so

calm? Didn't she know what was about to happen? She kept on looking at him, and then he understood. She wanted to go. He felt like shaking her. Didn't she know this was the end? The end of their dreams? Last night, they had almost married. Now, they were both about to die. And she was glad.

What is it, Hannah? What do you know that I don't? How can you be so calm? The executioner marched up to the platform and raised his rifle to Hannah's chest. Simon would never have the chance to ask her.

***

Hannah studied the executioner and took a breath to calm herself. The music had faded away, but her sense of hearing was still heightened, as if she could detect every breath, every movement, every rustle of the prisoners who waited for her death. Another breeze whispered past her.

"I've crossed over Jordan to Canaan's fair land."

She caught Simon staring at her. Although her heart was fuller than ever before, his look sent a sharp pang through her chest. *Lord, give him strength to watch me fall.* The speaker lectured the crowds, and she asked God one last time for forgiveness and grace.

"I've heard the sweet music, that heavenly song."

The speaker scowled. "The prisoner will be silenced or gagged," he barked. Hannah hardly understood his words. Had she been singing out loud? The corners of Simon's eyes crinkled slightly. His off-key baritone rose up to join her.

"From glory land over the sea, a soul-thrilling message from Jesus, our Lord."

Another man joined their chorus. She didn't need to look out at the crowds to recognize Mal-Chin's voice. For a moment, her singing faltered. Mal-Chin was elderly. She had tended to him in the infirmary once. His body might not withstand another beating.

"I will sing, I will praise you, worship my God, my King." He and Simon sang the next line without her.

"Silence," the speaker commanded, but his hand holding the megaphone trembled slightly.

The wind picked up, slapping strands of hair across her face. As more and more voices joined in, she knew not even death would silence their music. She waited. Any second, a bullet would lodge itself in her heart, but the praise would continue. The revival had already started. And the National Security Agency was powerless to stop it.

"I will shout, 'Hallelujah.'"

"Now!" the speaker yelled to the guard, who had lowered his rifle to the level of Hannah's knees. "Do it!" At first, the executioner made no indication he had heard. The speaker shouted again, and the guard raised his weapon once more.

"This is like heaven to me."

She kept singing. She wouldn't fear anybody ever again. Her death today would pave the way for thousands of Koreans to witness the grace and glory of God. What greater honor could she hope for in this life?

"Do it!"

The executioner moved his thumb across the rifle's mechanism.

Forgive him, Father.

He shut his left eye to aim.

"No!" Simon's voice carried over the noise of the crowd. He rushed forward, a gray streak charging toward her. She braced herself. She tried to warn him, but her voice caught in her throat.

The shot rang out. Simon fell. His blood splattered across the platform and pooled at Hannah's bare feet.

CHAPTER 36

She dropped to her knees beside him and stifled a sob. Her hands were still bound, so she couldn't even prop his head up. The front of his uniform shirt grew darker every second. "Simon?" She laid her body next to his, nuzzling her face against his cheek. "Can you hear me?" He stared back at her with lifeless eyes. Her uniform soaked up the puddle of blood on the platform. She didn't care. Her blood would soon mix with his. The speaker stopped shouting. The crowd ceased their singing. Hannah's ears rushed with echoes of roaring silence. She propped herself up to kiss Simon's clammy forehead. She only hoped to join him now in heaven. What was the executioner waiting for?

"What are you trying to prove, killing a little girl?" The shout came from the center of the throng but carried all the way to the platform. The prisoner's angry voice was met with murmurs of agreement. "How's her death supposed to honor the Eternal President, unless he's a blood-thirsty ..."

Three rapid shots silenced his protest. Several women shrieked. A scuffle. More shouts. The stomp of boots squelching in the muddy ground. It was all background noise as Hannah leaned her head on Simon's shoulder. *I want to go home with you. Please. Tell God I'm ready. I just want to be together. Forever this time.*

She shut her eyes, and a single tear streamed down her cheek. Another rifle shot sounded, but it came nowhere near her. She looked out. In the center of the gathering, the crowd had tried to part, and now a dozen more guards descended on the area. The whole mass undulated in a terrifying rhythm, but Hannah still didn't understand.

"Silence them!" The grumbling grew to a collective, outraged roar. A few more people screamed. Like ants scurrying from a flooded hill, the prisoners did what they could to scatter, but the sea of bodies surrounding them proved an impassable barricade. By the time the next wave of rifle fire rang out, half of the guards were in the middle of the fray, and the others stood ready along the outskirts of the crowd.

Hannah's stomach churned. She closed her eyes and lowered her head to Simon's. *I just want to go home with you.*

Something touched her shoulder. She jumped. "They'll kill you too." Mal-Chin's gnarled fingers tugged at the rope around her wrists.

The horde continued pressing out, swallowing up the guards who stood on the circumference of the gathering. Dozens of shots sounded over the screams and protests of the mob in grotesque syncopation, and Hannah saw more National Security agents racing in with machine guns. Mal-Chin pulled her down behind the platform. "Come on. Follow me."

Hannah paused. "Simon ..."

"He would want you to live." Mal-Chin had to yell to be heard. "Let's go!"

He ducked down and yanked her after him. Just seconds later, the first bursts of machine-gun fire splattered through the air. More shrieks. Hannah tried to look back, but Mal-Chin kept pulling her, keeping her up with a shocking display of strength when her feet stumbled beneath her. Her heart raced so fast she thought she might almost swallow it. He didn't stop even when the barbed wire came into view, but Hannah slowed down instinctively. The fence was at least half a meter taller than he. There was no way they could scale it.

"Trust me," Mal-Chin shouted over his shoulder. "It's the only way."

Hair lashed against her cheeks, and her legs threatened to collapse beneath her, but Mal-Chin kept rushing forward. She couldn't even find the breath to warn him it was electric. Just two steps away from the looming barricade, he wrapped both hands around her waist.

"No. Please, don't!" she shouted, but there was too much momentum for either of them to stop. He hoisted her up, roared loudly from exertion, and jumped, propelling her into the air.

His body fell forward. Hannah heard the awful electric hiss as soon as his hands released her. She waved her arms and legs wildly, scraping both shins on the barbs on top of the fence. She tumbled over and landed on her stomach. The fall sucked her breath out of her, but when she could finally gasp again, there was only the stench of burnt flesh. She forced herself to look back.

Mal-Chin's body slumped against the wires, burn marks etched across his expressionless face. Smoke drifted up from his hands and neck, and the occasional sizzle from the fence was more deafening than the machine-gun fire they left behind.

"Mal-Chin?" she whispered faintly, even though she knew there would be no response.

It was several minutes before her brain registered that she was outside the camp. She was free. Hannah's mind told her to get moving. It didn't matter where. As soon as the guards got the protest under control, they would invade the woods looking for any who escaped. She had seen enough of torture and jail cells to last a lifetime. But could she really just walk away? She wanted to reach out to Mal-Chin, to take the old man's hand in hers, but she was afraid to reach through the wire. Had he known all along? Even if he had survived, there would have been no way for him to join her on the other side.

Her throat constricted. How many men had died on her account today? In the distance, machine-gun fire still pierced the air with its deadly staccato. A clap of thunder sounded overhead, and a slight drizzle wet her cheeks. How much rain would it take to wash Simon's blood off that platform, to cover the violence taking place near the administration building right now? Would the rain cool down Mal-Chin's charred body? What had God been thinking? She was ready to die. Ready to go home. Why hadn't he let her complete her mission? And what was she supposed to do now? She hadn't been outside in months. She tried to guess where the sun was behind the clouds. She didn't even know which direction was which. And if she did, what would that change? Simon's body was back in the camp. Mal-Chin was here, his scarred, burnt flesh tangled in the fence. She couldn't just leave them, could she?

The whole mission from start to finish was botched. Even Mr. Tong, her only successful delivery, had been killed. That was probably her fault as well. Branches ripped at her cheeks. She was several paces away from the fence before she even realized she was running. She had no idea how she would travel, but there was only one place for her now. Simon and Mal-Chin and all the prisoners shot in the mob would remain in North Korea, probably tossed in some mass grave, but this wasn't her home.

Not anymore.

She wiped her face, struggling to hold back her sobs. There would be time for tears later. For now, she had to get back across the Tumen. She had to get to Yanji.

She was going home to the Sterns.

PART 5

CHAPTER 37

Juliette sat down at her computer. Still no email from her daughter. Kennedy was scheduled to take her last final today. Had she studied enough? Would she still have time to pack her things for the long flight back to Yanji?

The house would be a lot quieter than Kennedy was used to. They didn't have any refugees living there anymore. The Chinese police were getting suspicious and had interviewed her husband on two different occasions. Juliette and Roger both agreed they needed to take some time away from such a dangerous ministry.

It was getting dark. Juliette glanced at the clock. Roger would be home soon. She would have to get dinner going before too long. After ten years relying on hired help to do all the meal prep and cooking for her, Juliette was glad to have the kitchen back to herself after their housekeeper left last fall. She took a sip of tea and thought about calling Roger to ask him what he'd like to eat. The two of them had a Scrabble game in the upstairs den left over from last night. Juliette would never admit it to her husband, but she had sneaked a peek at an online dictionary and had a twenty-four point move all mapped out.

The doorbell rang. She refreshed her browser one last time to make sure Kennedy hadn't emailed her in the past ten seconds, and then she headed to the entryway. She peered through the peep hole, threw back the lock, and flung the door open with a gasp. "What in the world ...?" She couldn't believe how much weight Hannah had lost in only half a year. She was so frail it felt like her bones might break if Juliette even hugged her.

A hundred questions whizzed through her mind as she ushered the child in. Why had she returned? What happened back in North Korea? There was so much she wanted to ask, but the poor girl looked shell-shocked. No, worse than shell-shocked. Shell-shocked, starving, and feverish all at the same time. Juliette led her to the couch and covered her up with a blanket. Her feet were bare, the skin cracked open. She wondered when Hannah lost the nice hiking boots they gave her. "Let's get you warmed up, darling. I have some tea right here."

Hannah winced as she drank, but within seconds the entire mug was empty.

"My goodness, pumpkin, when was the last time you ate? No, don't answer that. I'll fix you up something right away. We have some bread rolls and salad in the fridge. Do you want more tea, too?"

A few minutes later, dinner plans completely forgotten, Juliette sat across from Hannah and put her hand on the girl's knee. "We'll get you more to eat in just a bit. You better let your poor stomach rest a little first." Juliette dabbed at her face with her sleeve. It wasn't hot outside, but the house sure had been sweltering lately. She would have to ask Roger to look at the furnace one of these days when he had the time. "You've been through a lot, sweetie. But I want you to know I'm so, so happy to see you." Part of Juliette was scared to learn everything Hannah had gone through. The poor thing was as thin as those pictures of Holocaust survivors. How could Juliette ever forgive herself for sending the poor child off alone?

Hannah mumbled something — the first words she had spoken since she arrived — and then put her hand to her mouth. Juliette thought she was about to throw up. She scurried to grab a bowl. "Are you feeling ill, sweetheart? Did you eat too much?"

Hannah stared straight past Juliette's shoulders. "Simon's dead."

Without a word, Juliette wrapped Hannah up in her arms and held the trembling child until Roger came home half an hour later.

***

Hannah glanced up from the garden bench when she heard the sliding door open. Mrs. Stern propped the tray on her hip and sauntered outside with a smile. "Ready for tea, angel?"

Hannah took the mug. After two weeks back at the Sterns', her palate still hadn't reacquired the taste for honey with her tea.

"It's a beautiful day." Mrs. Stern reached down to pluck a weed and then sat down next to Hannah on the bench. "Maybe you'd like to take a nap in the hammock this afternoon."

"No." She hadn't meant to snap. She offered Mrs. Stern an apologetic half-smile. "I mean, I still get a little chilled outside."

Mrs. Stern fanned herself with her hand. "Wish I could say the same thing. I'm burning up these days." She pointed to the Bible on Hannah's lap. "What are you reading?"

"Isaiah." She shut the book. How long ago had she and Simon discussed those same passages right here on this bench? She thought going back to the Sterns would make things easier, but there were so many memories in this place, mocking reminders of what she would never share with him again. She didn't know where else to go, but she couldn't stay here. Not with his ghost plaguing her every hour of the day. It was bad enough she couldn't sleep without seeing his blood flowing like a stream on the wooden platform.

Mrs. Stern stood up hastily. "I almost forgot. I made us some cookies." She waddled inside and came back out with a whole tray. "Chocolate chip. Help yourself."

Hannah took one and nodded her thanks without nibbling it. Didn't Mrs. Stern understand she just wanted to be alone? The days were so long, and she was so tired. Whenever she shut her eyes, she relived Simon's murder all over again. When she woke up in the morning, she felt the wet stickiness of his blood on her clothes. Other times, her mind replayed the smell of burnt flesh and made Hannah so nauseated she lost her appetite for the whole day.

She stared at the hammock. It had taken her several weeks to stumble up to the border, and even then she would have never made it to Yanji if a journalist hadn't bought her the bus ticket. It was days after she first arrived before Hannah could tell Mrs. Stern that Simon was killed by an executioner. She didn't mention he died saving her life. She didn't talk about Mal-Chin, either. As far as Mrs. Stern knew, Hannah had escaped during a prison uprising all by herself.

Last week, Mrs. Stern gave her a journal. She said it might help if Hannah wrote down her experiences, but the hundreds of crisp, unblemished pages intimidated her so much she never even opened it. She knew the Sterns were worried about her. She often heard them late at night talking. She couldn't make out the words but recognized the strain and worry in their voices. A few times they asked Hannah what she wanted to do next. They brought up South Korea or the United States, but the conversations left her so exhausted it took several days for her to recover enough strength just to get out of bed. Eventually, they stopped talking about the future, at least in front of Hannah. All Mrs. Stern seemed capable of conversing about lately was the weather or her frequent hot flashes.

"I'll have to ask Mr. Stern to fix the air conditioning before summer hits us," Mrs. Stern announced. A gentle breeze wafted by and rocked the empty hammock. "You really don't feel hot?"

Around the corner, they heard the gate close shut. Mrs. Stern frowned. "I wonder who that is. Roger's up in the den." She stood up and strained her neck. "Maybe you should go inside, sweetie," she whispered, "just to be safe."

"Hello?"

Hannah jumped off the bench. Suddenly dizzy, she reached out to steady herself on Mrs. Stern's shoulder. Mrs. Stern grasped her by the wrist. "Honey, are you all right? You look like ..."

"Mr. Stern?" The voice was closer now. Hannah heard him as he rounded the last bend into the garden. Her breath escaped her as soon as he came into view. His arm was wrapped in a sling, and he walked with his back hunched over. He stopped when he saw her. Dirt and blood caked onto his skin so it looked almost black. She tried to whisper his name, but her throat failed her. He was so frail. If she ran to him, she might knock him over. She felt her limbs trembling, but they refused to move toward him.

"Simon?" Mrs. Stern asked. Her voice squeaked once. "Is that really you?"

A sob from deep inside Hannah's gut came roaring to the surface. Her legs collapsed beneath her, and she sank back down onto the bench. He called her name and closed the distance between them in just a few short strides. He knelt in front of her and buried his head in her lap. "Hannah." He sobbed her name over and over, covering her hands with his kisses and tears. She stroked his matted hair with trembling fingers.

"You're alive?" she squeaked.

He was laughing and crying at the same time. "Barely."

The sliding door opened. "I thought I heard someone calling. Is everything ..." Mr. Stern stopped in the doorway. "Simon? We thought ..."

Simon wiped his face dry, smudging dirt on his cheeks, and stood up. "Mr. Stern." His voice squeaked. "Mr. Stern," he tried again. "You're a missionary."

"Yes. But do you care to tell us how you ..."

Simon squeezed Hannah's hand so hard it felt like he might break all her bones. "That makes you a minister then, right?" Hannah choked back something that was as much a laugh as a sob.

"I guess so," Mr. Stern answered tentatively, "but why does…"

Mrs. Stern stood up. "Hold on. It looks like the boy hasn't eaten in weeks. Let me get him a snack, and then you can ask him your questions."

"Not yet." Simon tugged on Hannah's hand and pulled her up to stand next to him. He wrapped his arm around her waist, and she felt his hip bone jutting out his side.

"You're about to fall over, darling," Mrs. Stern insisted. "At least let me go in and fix you up …"

"Juliette," her husband interrupted, "I think this young man was about to say something."

"Well, he should at least have a cookie." She held the platter up to Simon's nose, but he ignored it.

"Mr. Stern, I have a favor to ask you."

Hannah noticed the smile in Mr. Stern's eyes. "Anything. But first, you tell me how you're standing here talking to us. Because I know for sure the Bible teaches there's no such thing as ghosts."

Simon was smiling too. "Fine, then. But you'll only get the short version for now. And no questions. Not until later."

"Deal."

Hannah wondered how Simon's skinny legs could even hold up his weight. She was terrified to let go for fear he might blow away with the wind and be lost again. "I was injured in a prison uprising. Hannah maybe told you that much."

"She said it was an execution." Mrs. Stern was still holding the cookie plate out. "Said you were shot."

"True." Hannah wondered if she could ever grow tired of listening to his voice. "Well, during the riot, one of the prisoners …" He looked at Hannah. "The one with the missing fingers. You remember him, right? He dragged me to safety. Kept me hidden. Got my bleeding to stop. Found a way for us to escape through a chink in the fence."

Mr. Stern crossed his arms. "That's all you're going to tell us, then?"

"I still think the boy should at least have a few cookies," Mrs. Stern muttered.

"I'll take a cookie soon, I promise." Simon grinned at Mrs. Stern, but she didn't remove the plate until he actually picked one up. "But before I eat or answer questions or do anything else, I have a favor to ask Mr. Stern. A big one."

"And what kind of favor would that be?"

"I came a long way," Simon explained. "A lot of miles. A lot of sleepless nights. And it wasn't for Mrs. Stern's cookies. Even though I'm sure they taste great," he added at her look of disapproval.

"Well if it wasn't for dessert, why did you come back here, Brother?" Mr. Stern was smiling just as wide as he had when his daughter graduated high school last year.

Simon took both of Hannah's hands in his own. "I came back for an amazing young woman. A woman whose heart for the lost and compassion for the hurting brings me to my knees in shame. I lost her before, and I don't intend on ever losing her again." Hannah stared into his eyes. They were shining with life. With promise. With love. Simon cleared his throat, and a grin spread across his scarred, grimy face. "The reason I came back was to make this girl my bride." Off to the side, Mrs. Stern gave a little chirp that sounded halfway like a squeal and halfway like a puppy whining. Simon brought his cheek to Hannah's. "If she'll have me, of course."

Hannah nestled her face into the spot between his chin and his uninjured shoulder. It was all bones now, but she knew with rest and Mrs. Stern's cooking, it would grow to be as soft and inviting as she always imagined.

"I prayed I'd find you here," Simon whispered. "On my way back, I had so many nightmares. I'd show up here, and you'd be gone. But then I decided that if that happened, I'd just keep looking for you until I died from exhaustion. I don't ever want to say good-bye to you again."

Hannah ran her hands across his face, his cheeks, his hair. "There are no good-byes in the kingdom of heaven."

"Does that mean you'll marry me?" Simon asked.

She hid her face in his chest and nodded.

Mrs. Stern sniffled noisily. Mr. Stern cleared his throat. "Well then, friends, who's ready for a wedding?"

CHAPTER 38

Simon couldn't take his eyes off her throughout the entire dinner. Mrs. Stern insisted on fixing a full feast in honor of their wedding. *Their wedding.* Had it really happened? He kept expecting to wake up again in a solitary confinement cell. What had he ever done to deserve such happiness?

The Sterns sent them up to bed shortly after they ate, and while Hannah took a bath, Simon crept into the den, thankful to find Mr. Stern alone.

"Why aren't you with your new wife? It's your wedding night, you know."

Simon's face heated up at the directness of Mr. Stern's question, but he reminded himself he'd have to get used to Westerners and their outspoken nature. He kept his eyes down, but his voice was steady. "I'd like to talk with you about America. About the church you mentioned earlier."

Mr. Stern's mouth hung open for just a moment. "America? You want to talk about America right now?"

Simon's blush deepened. "It's just that ... we're married now," he tried to explain, but Mr. Stern interrupted.

"That's absolutely right. So why aren't you in bed right now with your bride?"

It was almost more than Simon could bear, but he forced himself to take a deep breath. "I want to make sure my wife is safe. And that means we can't stay here and impose on your hospitality indefinitely. The police ..."

"Yes, the police." Mr. Stern's voice turned serious and low.

He gestured for Simon to sit down. "As it turns out, Brother, we probably will have to find a new home for you soon."

Simon leaned forward in his chair.

"When it was just Hannah here, we didn't have the heart to send her away or scare her unnecessarily," Mr. Stern explained. "But we've been questioned. More than once." Simon nodded but felt guilty that he was too concerned about finding a safe place for Hannah to fret much about the Sterns and their situation. Mr. Stern rubbed the back of his head. "Since you've brought it up, I want you to know it's already something I've considered. In fact, I took the liberty of emailing that church in the States to see if they still needed a Korean pastor."

Simon nodded. He wondered if married life would always involve this flood of worries over his bride and suddenly grew pensive. "You don't think ..." He frowned as he tried to collect his thoughts. "You don't think it would be taking the coward's way out, do you?" He held his breath.

Mr. Stern patted Simon's knee. "Brother, if my wife or I went through half of the trials you or Hannah did, I can guarantee we'd be begging God for a plane ticket out of here. Sometimes you jump right into the fiery furnace because you know that's where the Lord's leading you, and sometimes you ..." Mr. Stern cleared his throat. Simon jumped to his feet. Even though he had just finished his first real meal in months, his knees felt weak.

Hannah stood at the doorway, her hair flowing down to her shoulders. She smiled shyly. "I wondered where you went."

Simon noticed the way she couldn't quite raise her eyes to meet Mr. Stern's, and he loved her all the more for it. He glanced at his mentor.

"You better get some rest," Mr. Stern told him. Simon couldn't be entirely sure in the dim light, but he thought Mr. Stern winked at him. "We can talk some more about it in the morning."

Hannah slipped her hand in his as they walked down the hall to the room. "Talk more about what?" At first, Simon tried to make up something petty to tell her. This was their wedding night, after all. He didn't want her worried about raids or repatriation or leaving Yanji. She stopped at the doorway and brushed his cheek with her finger. After everything she had suffered, he wondered how her skin could still feel so soft. He reached up to hold her and winced as his shoulder protested from the pain. She put her arm around his waist.

Soft and strong.

Her gaze was penetrating. Simon knew he couldn't hide the truth. "I was talking to Mr. Stern about where we should go from here." He waited for Hannah to respond, but she was frozen at the threshold of the room, staring at the bed. He felt a quiet tremor run through her body. He took his gnarled, calloused finger and tilted her chin up toward his face. "I love you," he whispered. "I want to take you someplace safe. Someplace where we'll never have to say good-bye again."

Her features softened, and she shut the door behind them.

***

The wind rustled through the garden. Simon took in a deep breath. How many times had he pictured it just like this in his dreams? How many days had he spent scaling impassable trails, his aching muscles fueled by visions of such bliss? It was all so perfect. Her head was resting on his uninjured shoulder, and even though her face was turned away, he could tell by her steady breathing she was asleep. Her. Hannah. His wife. Could it really be?

He thought about yesterday morning, when that journalist offered to pay his fare the rest of the way to Yanji. All the young red-head wanted in exchange was for Simon to answer a few questions about life back home. Simon didn't tell him much. He didn't even mention he escaped from the gulags. Still, the journalist seemed thrilled to have a real-life refugee to interview, and Simon got his ticket to Yanji. To her. He could still recall her face exactly as she looked when he came around through the back gate.

The hammock swayed, and he nuzzled the back of her neck. Was it really just a few weeks ago they were both condemned to death? It felt as if he was waking up from a strange dream. He still hadn't told her everything about his escape from camp and his journey north. Even over dinner last night, Simon had been too overwhelmed to share all of his story, but for the first time since he met Hannah, he realized he didn't have to rush. He would tell her everything eventually. They had all the time in the world together. There would be no more good-byes.

As Hannah dozed next to him, Simon regretted that he had to get up soon. A friend of Mr. Stern, a physician, was stopping by to look at Simon's bullet wound. Simon kissed the back of Hannah's neck, and she stirred beside him. "Are you awake?" he whispered.

She rolled over to face him, and a pang, sharper than anything he had experienced in Camp 22, pierced his heart. How could he protect her now that she had entrusted herself wholly to him? How could he keep from letting her down? How could he keep from failing?

Hannah smiled at him, and he kissed the tip of her petite nose. The garden door slid open, and they both scurried to sit up in the hammock, untangling themselves from the netting and from each other. Mrs. Stern came outside balancing a paper fan and a tall glass of lemonade in one hand and a plate of brownies in another. "Mr. Stern asked me to tell you the doctor's here for your shoulder," she told Simon. "And you, sweetie ..." She sat down in the bench across from Hannah and smiled slyly. "I thought you might want a little snack. Nothing works up an appetite like honeymooning."

Simon didn't have to look at his wife to guess the shade of red creeping into her cheeks. He and Hannah both stood at the same time, and he touched the back of her shoulder. "I'll be back soon," he whispered.

"I'll be here waiting."

"There's no hurry, darling," Mrs. Stern called after him. "A girl's got to eat to keep up her energy, you know."

He glanced at Hannah's timid smile, and for a moment he faltered. He didn't want to leave her for even a few minutes. Then he remembered. This was forever. When Mr. Stern joined their lives in marriage, it wasn't so they could spend a little time together again before they headed out for their next mission. No, this was different. This time, there would be no more good-byes.

Behind them both, the empty hammock rocked gently in the breeze.

ACKNOWLEDGEMENTS

Torn Asunder couldn't have been written and published without the prayers, encouragement, and practical support of a whole team.

My thanks go out to my story editor, Nat Davis, and copy editor, Sheila Hollinghead. I appreciate the professional thoroughness you both bring to each project you've helped me with. I also relied heavily on feedback from my beta readers, and am exceptionally grateful for the advanced reviewers and bloggers who helped me spread the word about my release. I'd like to especially mention Annie Douglas Lima, who consistently goes beyond the call of duty when it comes to the thoroughness of her beta reading.

Regi McClain, as always, offered support in a wide variety of ways. She is my critique partner as well as my prayer partner, who doubles as an editorial assistant and helps me tremendously with her amazing organizational skills. I'd also like to thank my other friends, those I've met in "real life" and those I haven't, who pray for me and my writing and bring so much encouragement. I would also like to mention Jon and Dabin and others who helped field my questions about Korean culture.

Cherie Norquay is an amazingly talented recording artist who was kind enough to let me use her lyrics in this novel. I was surprised time and time again by how perfectly her words fit in with everything Hannah and Simon went through. She is truly blessed and anointed by the Holy Spirit, and I love the way her lyrics give Hannah a true voice.

My husband remains my biggest fan and supporter. I am so thankful the Lord allowed us to enjoy such sweet romance and companionship. There is no way I could have written Hannah and Simon's story if I hadn't already known the thrill of being loved by someone so wonderful.

With each book I work on, I'm reminded of my own weaknesses. While writing *Torn Asunder*, carpal tunnel flare-ups and frequent eye strain reminded me I couldn't draft a single word if the Lord wasn't the one sustaining me. Additionally, the spiritual and emotional toil of getting a novel edited and ready to publish would be insurmountable barriers if the Lord didn't go before me and allow me to complete one more book.

Torn Asunder is dedicated to the brave men and women from North Korea who sneak back home to share the gospel and those who live out their faith in the most hostile mission field on earth. May the Lord protect and provide for all your needs, and may your stories continue to encourage and inspire us as you bring the gospel to people living in darkness and oppression.